Plentiful

by Alan Nelson

Andrew Benzie Books

Published by Andrew Benzie Books
www.andrewbenziebooks.com

Printed in the United States of America

Second Edition: August 2014

10 9 8 7 6 5 4 3 2 1

ISBN 978-1-941713-03-7

DOGGEREL BONES
MULTIPLEX

Cover image courtesy of www.freeimages.co.uk

Dedicated to Nina

CHRISTINA

They say the Parquat River
Is the Eighth Wonder of the World,
Running and curling between two cities,
An axe cutting a sweet apple in two.

It's said, somewhere on the eastside
There's a street without division,
But nobody's found that dream yet.
And somewhere on the westside
There's a man without influence,
But on that I'll never bet.

See, I'm a good Christian boy
Oh, a righteous Christian boy
And I've done what I've been taught.
But I read in the Good Book
How Christ threw the tables down,
And I keep hearing that debacle
From the tabernacle,
The cries of outrage
As Christ throws the tables down.

They say the Parquat River
Is the Eighth Wonder of the World,
There only to keep people apart—but bridges
Bridges keep people apart.

So grind cider for the Revo—"

"Christina, are you singing?"
I jumped inside. I didn't think my boss, Nicole, could hear me.
"Naw, just hummin to myself."
"You're always humming."

1

"So?"

"Hello . . . you have a customer."

I knew that. I was just waiting, ta da, ta da, ta da, for the weird lady to make her decision. While a bunch of people stood in line at the counter, she pondered the daily Kenyatta Koffee Klub question on the chalkboard above the pastries: What was Montgomery Clift's last film?

I checked out her funky skin, the ugly moles and sunspots on her arms, the diamond earrings, the silk blouse. Little games with rich people, I thought. I'm sooo glad this whole thing is about to end.

"I know the answer to that," she said. "Wasn't it about horses?"

I shook my head. "Sorry, I gotta have more than that to put your name in the cookie jar."

Nicole handed me a bagel plate with little containers of cream cheese and raspberry jam and I gave it to the woman. I was so tired I couldn't remember if she'd paid or not. Nicole wasn't looking, so I decided she had.

"Just a little hint?"

"My lips are sealed," I said, trying to smile but yawning instead.

"Can we move along?" a voice said, real impatient-like. It was the man standing second in line.

"I'm sorry, I guess I'm still sleepy," the lady apologized, stepping away with her food. "I'll try tomorrow."

"Great idea," the man said, stepping around her. "It's always best to think things over."

He set down one of those shiny black briefcases, then looked me right in the eye, shaking his head in frustration. He was on the short side, with a seriously trimmed beard, his eyes either blue or green or some ocean color, it was hard to tell. While the other customers were floating around in a Saturday morning daze, this guy was flashing a suit and tie like he was ready for action.

"It was *The Misfits*," he said, checking out the menu board. "You probably don't remember the film, you're too young, but it was terribly depressing. Forget about Montgomery Clift, it was Marilyn and Clark's last film as well."

What is this guy talking about? I wondered.

"Beats me," I said, "but cool, you're in the drawing for a free lunch." I handed him a pen to write his name on the stick-em pad.

He waved me off. "No, don't worry about it. I'd like two double lattes, each with extra cinnamon."

As I started banging the grounds into the can, Nicole walked up next to me.

"Anybody need just regular coffee?" she called out, then whispered, "Christina, pick it up a little, there's a slew of people standing around."

I smiled, then slyly thought: sure, I'll pick it up, but—surprise!—you're gonna be solo tomorrow.

So I started doing what I'd already done twenty-five times that morning: plunging the hissing nozzle into the milk to get it hot and gurgling; packing new coffee and fitting the discs into the machine; waiting for the magic juice to leak down into the little gravy boats, dumping them, then filling the cups with foamy white liquid. When I first got the job three months ago this machine had totally freaked me out, but now I could make shots in my sleep (which I felt like I was doing!).

"Here's your jolts of joy," I said, setting the tall cups on the glass counter.

"That looks dangerous," he said. "Could you put them in a bag for me?"

"I was afraid you were gonna say that," I mumbled.

"Well, you might have asked me about it to begin with, am I right?"

People in Falmouth, they were so on my nerves. I wanted to tell the man, Screw off, Mr. Briefcase, but I held my tongue out of guilt. I put the lattes in a bag like a good girl, then made his change.

"What does that tattoo say?" he asked, talking about my right bicep.

"Born to Lose."

He picked up his briefcase. "Quite a slogan," he said, then walked out.

I thought: Jesus, please forgive me, but *F* you!

"Why don't you just call it a shift," Nicole said, as if she'd heard my thoughts.

"But I need my check first," I said.

"Not until tomorrow."

"Come on. It's late again?" I complained, shrugging my shoulders, but really just pretending.

"Let's not broadcast our problems to the public, alright?" Nicole preached in her best snotty voice.

Whatever . . . Since this was the special day I would be meeting my friends and leaving for the mountains forever, it didn't really matter what fell outta her mouth anyway.

Nicole opened the register, lifted out the cash drawer and handed it to me, sliding in a replacement.

"Just set it on the safe. I'll get to it when it dies down out here. But I'll need you here again tomorrow morning at 6:30. And be sure to put the bags of trash in the dumpster when you leave. You forgot yesterday."

"Sure thing," I answered obediently. I took the tray through the swinging doors into the kitchen. Lord, forgive me for what I'm gonna do, but I know You understand it's for a higher good.

I set the drawer of money on the top of the safe, so majorly frightened I felt numb. I carefully checked over my shoulder: Nicole was talking with a customer, busy with the espresso machine. I picked up the packet of big bills—the tens and twenties—and stuffed them in my pants pocket, then made sure to get four quarters for the bus ride across the river to Circleville. I left some scattered bills to make it look like the right money was still there. As I opened the back door of the shop, I murmured Nicole's favorite training mantra under my breath—Remember, good service starts with a smile—then split.

The patio outside was crowded with tables and all the people I'd just served. I avoided their evil eyes and skipped down the shopping center steps, then walked fast along the sidewalk towards the bus stop, trying not to look like a criminal. Feeling the bulging money, I just *knew* C.W. was gonna be proud of my contributions to the community.

Out beyond the parking lot, rising up above the busy intersection, was the shiny Eugenia Flowers Memorial Hospital. The trees surrounding the glass buildings were turning yellow and orange, doing their October thing. That hospital was where Ralph Borbon died last year after the church riots. C.W. had held a candlelight vigil in front of the place when he was getting treatment there. When I visited him his whole body was bandaged up like a mummy.

Then I noticed a weird little whirlwind starting up at the far end of the parking lot. I watched it out of curiosity cause I'd always been kinda amazed at how the wind could come together like that. It disappeared for a sec, then started spinning stronger and stronger, leaves and trash jumping in the air like little puppets on invisible strings.

But then I just stopped in my tracks when I noticed the last customer I'd served—the smart-ass man with the briefcase—was walking out to his car, heading right towards the twister. Everything happened so fast that I didn't have time to warn the guy, but, zap, it was suddenly all around him, catching him in all the flying junk. He jerked forward to hide his face, letting go of the briefcase and dropping the bag I'd just given him inside—the coffee splashing all over the asphalt. Then, as quickly as it hit him, the whirlwind zig-zagged away.

The poor dude went ballistic, yelling out and kicking the ground. He peeled a piece of paper off his pant leg and tossed it away. I just stood there giggling. Served him right.

He hurried over to his car and slammed the door shut as he got inside. When he drove by me, he was looking at his watch, about to blow a gasket. But I noticed he drove the coolest silver Jag, just like the wheels CEO Forsythe used to drive at the cannery.

Lucky for me, I also saw the bus coming down Bridgeway Drive and ran to catch it.

Trajan and the others would be waiting at the agreed spot at 17th and Bingham.

But dear Jesus, just thinking about the escape plan—and seeing Trajan—made my stomach hurt big-time.

BARBARA

It was always the same issue, Where was my boss? I could never understand it, I was never late, so why was he always, predictably, tardy, wreaking havoc in the schedule? It was like a personal slight inflicted time and again that he paid no attention to. And, of course, my being worried stiff meant my cuticles suffered in the worst way; I'd rubbed so hard that both my thumbs had that terrible paper-cut feeling. The morning appointments were already in a shambles—Ah, there he is!

As Dr. Merrithew stepped out of the fifth floor elevator, I quickly stood up from my desk and followed him into the waiting area.

"Good morning," I said, hiding my frustration.

"Hello Barbara, have the savages gathered yet?"

"Yes, they're inside," I said, noticing the front of his suit was a mess. "What happened to you?" I gasped.

"I spilled coffee all over myself. Let's not go into it."

"Can I do something?"

"No, don't worry about it."

"OK, if you say so. You do know that surgery was changed to 11:30, don't you?"

"Right. A belly tuck?"

"Yes."

"Any messages?"

"There's quite a stack of them on your desk."

"Any news on the big fish?"

"Affirmative," I answered proudly. I'd phoned Florence, Italy the previous day and made arrangements for the special surgery, which had been no easy task.

"Well?"

"She's coming!"

Dr. Merrithew smiled, then, without so much as a thank you for a job well done, he turned and walked away to his office. I followed behind, stopping in my cubicle on the way to pick up my notebook and Blackberry organizer. When I entered his office he was pulling a thick packet of papers out of his briefcase.

"Chopped down another tree, I see."

"Yes, I'm afraid so."

He put the papers into proper reading position, then took off his coat and placed it over the back of the brown leather chair. I sat down in one of the red armchairs facing his desk, toying with my pencil.

"Estelle phoned you. She said to call her immediately, it was very important."

Dr. Merrithew's forehead pinched. "When did she call?"

"Just before you got here," I answered. "I didn't know your wife was flying to Chicago this week. And, as I'm sure you're aware, with a traveling companion by the name of Jackson."

His mind seemed to go blank. "I just left her—we finished talking," he said oddly, more to himself than me.

"Well, it sounded important, whatever it was."

He didn't sit down, but instead moved over to the big window and gazed at the hospital grounds, rubbing his hands, distracted. "You know the paintings that Estelle put up last week?" he asked out of the blue. "They clash with the gold carpeting. Did you notice that?"

"Well, I wouldn't know, you're a better art connoisseur than I am." I noticed his spotted pants again. I told him to wait a moment and rushed out of the office and came back with a couple of hand towels from the rest room.

"Here let me help you," I said, kneeling down and rubbing his pant leg.

"You're a sweetheart, Barb, but you shouldn't get in that position—think of what the staff would think."

"Stop it, Dr. Merrithew, you're embarrassing me," I said, standing up. "What about your hands?" He spread his hands out and I rubbed them down vigorously.

He laughed. "Go ahead, claim harassment. What's a little more litigation anyway, right?"

It annoyed me when he talked provocatively like that, so I just ignored his remarks and neatly folded the towels and brushed down my pantsuit. "Are you ready? We're late."

"Sure. From one sticky situation to another."

So, finally, we got down to clinic business and walked over to the surgical unit where the conference room was located.

Dr. Merrithew's two business partners, Dr. William Stratton and Dr. Sadiq Halim, were already waiting when we came in, each spread out on their respective sides of the long mahogany table.

"Where's the new anesthetist?" Dr. Merrithew asked.

"She's not coming today. We thought it would be best to meet alone," Dr. Stratton said.

"Is that so," Dr. Merrithew answered. "Are things that bad, the waiting rooms deserted?"

"No, I wouldn't say that, there's just a need for some privacy," Dr. Stratton said, tapping his pen on a pad of paper. Dr. Merrithew used to comment—and it never failed to make me laugh—that Dr. Stratton was living proof that Human Character was best reflected in the human face. He would say, I'll leave it to you to determine what this guy is all about, what with his chin like a car bumper, his pink nose, and his broken malicious smile.

"What's the first order of business?" Dr. Merrithew asked.

"I'm sure Barbara has an agenda," Dr. Halim said.

"Yes, I do," I said, putting my glasses on, "but first: Dr. Merrithew, do you want some coffee?"

"No, after hearing Bill's ominous introduction, I'm as wide awake as the meeting demands."

"I won't touch that one," Dr. Stratten said wearily, clearing his throat. "Let's get rolling."

I straightened my posture, opened my notebook, and glanced at the Blackberry screen through my bifocals, knowing it was going to be one of *those* meetings. From my lap, I rubbed my cuticle again, the stinging improving my concentration.

"Mr. Bierne, the attorney on the Duffield case, phoned," I said.

"Well, it's about time," Dr. Merrithew complained.

"Yes, he'll be phoning back. According to the court calendar, the trial will begin on December 15th, possibly a week sooner."

"What's the status of that case, Collin?" Dr. Halim asked. "I think when we last talked it had been continued."

"Everything and nothing," Dr. Merrithew said. "Things are stuck in the standard glacial processes of the courts," he said, taking a deep breath. "Bierne got me the copy of my depo, but I haven't had time to read it yet. It's a case I have to give considerable thought to—"

"I would hope so," Dr. Stratton noted dryly.

Dr. Merrithew paused. "I'm so very, very glad we agree on that. Can I continue?"

"By all means."

"The plaintiff's attorney has gone back to New York and hired a psychiatric expert, Dr. Martin Segelman, who is a prominent hired gun at Yale, so this whole thing is . . . it's out of hand. I have to talk with Bierne about what moat and castle walls we need to start building for our defense."

"What's her condition now?" Dr. Halim queried.

"Subjectively, she's still having a great deal of pain," Dr. Merrithew said. He seemed to reach for a cup of coffee that wasn't there, and I felt a pang of responsibility. "Bierne's independent medical examiner was a bit wishy-washy in his opinions, and, of course, they have a life care specialist who say's she can no longer take care of the house, her kids, pour Corn Flakes, whatever, due to the depression."

"Is she still an inpatient?"

"In and out, the last I heard."

Dr. Stratton stirred in his seat then cleared his throat again. "You know, this whole affair makes me think we should really take a closer look at our protocol with patients."

"God damn it, we've been around and around about this," Dr. Merrithew said, annoyed. "I operated three times, with some scarring, yes, but generally excellent results. I don't know why she's acting this way. She's basically a nut case. I'll be blunt, she wanted to be a *Bay Watch* babe—a 38 CC cup celebrity—and her ideal wasn't achieved."

"Well, that's an amusing slant on a disastrous mammoplasty," Dr. Stratton said.

Dr. Merrithew slapped the table with both hands, startling me. "Bill, I'm bad with a knife, I repent. And I regret increasing your income three hundred thousand dollars this past year—"

"Collin, take it easy," Dr. Halim interrupted. "We all appreciate the business you bring to the Institute, and our growing reputation, but Bill has a point, this deserves more discussion. The Duffield case goes beyond your office and practice. In the past two years we've had four complaints made to the State Board and two lawsuits, and they've all landed on your plate. Although we know some of these have been outlandish claims, Duffield is a mess and has leaked into the local media."

"That's good publicity," Dr. Merrithew teased.

"Come on, be serious," Dr. Halim complained.

"I am, Sadiq. When it all blows over, the name remains. That's the bottom line."

"Can I say something?" Dr. Stratton asked. "We need to consider the red flags more—"

"You sound like you're teaching a nursing seminar," Dr. Merrithew remarked in disbelief. "What—a Rorshach at the pre-op consultation?"

"Children, please," Dr. Halim pleaded. He stood up and moved over to the window, putting his hands behind his back. "Collin, Bill doesn't want About Face to become some mega-liposuction farm, which is the direction we're heading."

Dr. Merrithew laughed. "For someone who's entire practice is devoted to—limited to—the use of a cannulla, I find that quite surprising."

"Shut up, Collin. That's unprofessional and I won't stand for it," Dr. Stratton said.

Dr. Merrithew just sat still, grinning, letting the tension mushroom. I never really understood it, but he seemed to relish the social anxiety that others avoided. I checked my watch and confirmed again what I already knew: Surgery was running behind schedule.

I glanced at Dr. Halim. He put his fingers to his lips, absorbed in the view outside. Sadiq was a handsome Indian, very dark-skinned, with brilliant white teeth and thick hair and bushy eye brows, and when he was concerned about something or wanted to make a point, he did so by dramatizing his own beauty.

He turned back, ready for oratory: "Let's think bottom line here. We should counter this whole wave of negative publicity by hiring a consultant to talk with us about our image problem."

"Just because of Duffield?" Dr. Merrithew asked, chuckling.

"That's right," Dr. Stratton followed up, "the whole set of liability issues is a prairie fire."

Just then, the phone on the conference table beeped. I excused myself and answered it. I took the message, then sat back in my chair. "Dr. Merrithew, it's your wife. She says it's urgent."

"O.K. Gentlemen, I sense a higher calling. Certainly none of us have time for this debate right now. The case may settle, but if not, I'll testify in December and the matter will be resolved, then, hopefully, with your kindly support and encouragement, we can move on. Is that alright with everyone?"

"No," Dr. Stratton answered. "But we can talk about it some other time."

After Dr. Halim agreed to postpone the discussion until the following week, the meeting ended.

Fifteen minutes later, I returned to Dr. Merrithew's office, carrying a latte I'd hurriedly bought at his favorite local espresso shop. He was reading the deposition.

"I thought you might like this after that inspired meeting," I said.

"You must have read my mind," Dr. Merrithew said. "I love it when a woman does that."

He lifted the lid of the drink and took a sip; there was no doubt about it, the man loved coffee and drank it constantly throughout the day.

"Bill always rises to the highest level of mediocrity when he opens his mouth, don't you think?" Dr. Merrithew smirked. "I suppose he can't help it, poor soul."

I sat down in front of his palatial desk, secretly sucking on a breath mint.

"Did I tell you how nice it is to gaze upon your elegant nose during these morning debates," Dr. Merrithew said.

"Doctor, don't be silly. As if you don't have more important things on your mind."

"Are you glad you had the procedure? I never asked you about it."

"Well, yes, after all the black and blue faded away."

He laughed, savoring another sip. "You mean, it *is* surgery after all?"

Why did he always ask me about that? It made me feel like a patient, and not the alluring she-devil that I wanted to be.

"Did you talk to Estelle?" I asked, daring to change the subject.

"No, not yet," he said, quickly closing the file.

"Won't she be leaving for the airport?"

"She will be shortly."

I stirred in my seat. I wanted to touch my nose, but was self-conscious about it now; I rubbed the burgundy-colored buttons on the chair instead. He was avoiding his wife, it was obvious, why, I had no idea. Maybe there was a real chance for me after all. Who was this Jackson anyway? I wanted to ask, but assumed I'd be prying.

"Let's get on to bigger and better things, particularly the one and only Ivanessa Magliori," he said.

"She's arriving from Rome on Monday," I said, opening my Blackberry to M.

"And?"

"She wants to have a consultation on Tuesday, and if all goes well, surgery later in the week. I talked with her manager, who is, I'm afraid, a little above my head. He's a very demanding gentleman with a thick accent. He said Ms. Magliori was quite impressed with you on the phone last week; she said you were sensitive to her special creative needs. Evidently, she plans to hold a press conference about the whole thing, then drive here. It sounds like she has an entourage of some sort."

"Really?" Dr. Merithew said with satisfaction, "That's great news. Give total priority to this. Cancel whatever appointments are necessary."

His request made me cringe; organizing appointments was so difficult that I hated the idea of changing *any* of them.

"I'll do my best," I said, "but I'm swamped."

"Barbara, come on, I need all your energy and help on this one."

I considered raising the salary issue, but, again, it seemed like bad timing with all the pressure he was dealing with, so I kept quiet. Dr. Merrithew glanced at the clock on the wall. He had to be in the medical suite in forty-five minutes.

"God, I haven't even looked at the information she sent us," he said. "Where is it?"

"The brown package next to your phone," I pointed out. He opened the box that I'd received from the famous avant-garde performance artist and movie star the week before, then pulled out the contents.

"Come here and look at this," he said.

I walked over and stood by his side at the desk. There was a letter, signed in a flourish by Ms. Magliori, and some 8 x 11 inch photographs.

"What are those?" I asked.

"Pictures. The models I'll work from." He held one up, examining it closely like an x-ray.

"Is that her?"

"Yes, just exquisite isn't she? Perfect bones," Dr. Merrithew gushed, shifting his chair for better light. I couldn't help but swoon myself, too envious to respond. He shuffled the pictures.

"You know the martyr, Joan of Arc, of course," Dr. Merrithew said.

"Sure," I answered. I'd seen the image—the armor, the lance, and young boyish face with short hair—a hundred times.

"And Botticelli's, *Venus on a Half Shell.*"

That face was also familiar.

"This person I don't know," Dr. Merrithew said. He looked at the back of an old, cracked black and white photograph. "It says, Nobel Prize-winning Italian poet, Grizana Morta." We both looked at the small image of a woman standing in front of a tree and water fountain.

"Not a beauty, but full of character," I said.

"An unfortunate forehead," Dr. Merrithew commented, spreading the four photographs out on his desk. He read the letter again, then put it aside. "Barbara, I need you to do a little computer work for me. Let me show you what I'm talking about."

"Doctor, I can't work overtime again today. I'm sorry, I just can't."

"Put that other stuff on hold."

That *other stuff* was work that had been put on hold before and was now on the front burner! Then I just blurted it out: "I can't keep working so much overtime without being compensated, Dr. Merrithew. It's not right and it's not fair."

Well, there it was, I finally got it off my chest.

He put the photograph down, then reached over and held my hand. It was the first time he'd ever touched me on purpose. I felt a jolt of desire to bend over and kiss his lips, but also repulsion at what was happening, and ended up just standing there rigid as a statue.

"I know you have important things you want to discuss," he said understandingly. He wasn't the most handsome man, but his hazel eyes, his voice, were fabulous at that moment. "But can't we talk about this next week, after this storm has passed? Is that too much to ask?"

I smiled weakly. "I'm sorry, I just lost it there for a moment. That wasn't right of me."

"It's no problem. It's good to express one's true feelings," he said, pressing my hand then quickly letting go. "But right now the emergency is Magliori, so let's get to it."

We moved over to the computer workstation, which was set in a ceiling-tall bookcase on the far side of the office. He sat down and spread out the photographs. I had to force myself to concentrate because even though he had touched me, even though I had stated my needs, I was shaking inside with helplessness.

"I need you to scan these photographs so that I can work with them," Dr. Merrithew said. "Is the scanner functional?"

"I think so," I responded. I picked up the photograph of Joan of Arc. "What are the shots going to be used for?"

"Ivanessa is requesting that her face be changed to incorporate the key elements of these three faces."

"I don't understand."

"She wants Joan of Arc's lips, Morta's eyes, Venus' chin."

"Like for real, literally?"

"Yes, as literally as possible—that's my job."

"My God, that's terrible," I protested, screwing up my lip. "Why?"

"I don't know why, frankly. Why ask why? She's an artist."

"It's strange, that's all," I complained, sounding whiney. I was embarrassed by my own naive sense of conviction, but I went on anyway: "Her face is on the cover of every magazine in the world as it is—wasn't she on Imperium last month? I guess I assumed she was getting some type of touch up or something, but to totally change, totally transform, her face, that's—"

"I understand what you're saying," the doctor interrupted. Leaving the photographs by the computer, he stood up. "It'll be some delicate, some very challenging, work; the typical puzzle, times three. And she wants to beam the entire procedure on the Internet—a complete multi-media depiction of the surgery."

"Well, none of this was shared with me."

"That's why we're talking, am I right? But Barb, the clinic has to be pretty much deserted, you understand? There's going to be a slew of technicians and artistic reps traipsing along with her, so there needs to be plenty of open space for her crew and Persona to expand into.

Talk to the partners and let them know. If they have any complaints, tell them this complex theatrical piece is being completed for half a million dollars. If they continue to whine, talk to me."

"That's what she's paying?" I asked, opening my eyes wide in surprise.

If I were in charge, she'd be prohibited from the whole affair. But who cares what I think? "I'll get to all this in the afternoon. Do you need another coffee?"

"No. Can you call surgery and tell them I'll be right down?"

"Sure thing."

I used the desk phone and called Kitty Wong, the anesthetist, who told me the patient would be late. There had been some disturbance in town—a robbery or something—that closed down the Concourse. I needed to phone the afternoon patient and inform her the procedure would be delayed. I hung up and told Dr. Merrithew. Any delay was worthwhile, he said, since it gave him a chance to read the Duffield deposition.

Then the phone rang again and I answered it. Ha, she's cornered him!

"It's Estelle," I said, tempted to listen in on another line.

"Barb, I need a minute alone."

"Sure, no problem. Anyway, I've got about a thousand things to do."

Waiting for someone to answer the phone, what a senseless void for the mind.

Looking out the bedroom window, down to the circular driveway, I watched Dolores pack my bags into the Audi, the dogs darting around her as if they were making the trip to Chicago too. After last night's exhausting pillow talk, I doubted Collin would answer the phone, and after two calls without a response, my fears were confirmed. But somewhere in the corner of my sleeping pill-bruised mind I was still hoping for some breakthrough, so here I was on the phone again.

I lay back in bed, hot and clammy, nausea passing through my stomach like a school of fish.

"Hello?" I heard Collin say.

"Hi, it's me."

"Barbara said you'd called."

"Yes, I did—more than once."

There was a long unfulfilled pause. He finally spoke up, "Well, anything I should know . . . other than what I already know?"

"Did you get my sister's cell phone number? I put it by your wallet."

"Just tell me. I'll remember it."

"332-988-8144. I put her address there too."

"Good," he said.

"I phoned just to . . . touch base one more—one last—time. I thought about everything you said and everything I said . . . I don't know, it seemed like, down deep, you were still confused about what you wanted to do. I—"

"No, you've got it wrong. I haven't changed my mind."

"Oh, Collin, you don't know yourself, you know that. For all your savvy upstairs, you just don't."

Was that a deep breath, maybe a rustle of paper, at the other end of the line? Was he even listening?

"Maybe I should wait a few more days," I said softly, carefully.

"Estelle, we've talked about this for weeks. You and I both know you're at a dangerous stage now. You can't wait."

"Dangerous? Now that's a twist."

"Please, stop trying to be so intuitive. Nothing's changed for me: same predicament, same solution."

"Stop it right there," I insisted. Through my fatigue, my blood was still boiling. I didn't want to argue just before the flight, but I couldn't help it. I felt so crappy, so empty. Was I even going to make it to Chicago? "After thirty-nine years on this earth, after ten years of marriage, you can't commit to it? Is that what you're saying?"

The royal silence. I waited, but nothing. Maybe I should just take all my pills—Ha, now that would be a surprise! Kill two birds.

"You know," I went on, "I'm sure this is all very redundant for you, but I'm sick of it too—"

"Estelle, wait, Barbara's talking to me."

Yes, more open space; I'm so sick of waiting. Where's your courage, your guts? Why wait for his fucking approval? Why wait for anything? I looked down to the Audi again, noticing for no reason a dent in the back fender. I wondered about that pretty Girl Friday, Dolores. She was very industrious. Was she part of the harem, or was there a harem? I didn't know and didn't much care.

"Estelle, you there?"

"Of course I'm here."

"But what's that sound?" he asked, off subject.

"I don't know. Dolores is vacuuming, if that's what you mean. Is it important?"

"No. Honey, I have to get back to work. You know I wish I could come with you, but right now there's just too much going on at the clinic."

"I know, that holy inviolable place—" No, no, stop right there, I told myself, no arguments before the flight. "I understand, I guess," I added in a calmer voice.

"You're back Thursday?"

"It depends on how things go, you know that."

"Sure."

"Collin, I'm scared. I'm freaked out by the whole thing."

"I'll phone you religiously, OK? We can talk about everything while you're going through it. Say hello to your family."

But every one of his words just aroused protest in me. "Collin!

Don't you want a little Jackson? Don't you? Come on, I'm home anyway."

"Like I said, I'll call you."

"I love you," I whispered, then added quickly in my thoughts: I despise you! But there was only a dial tone . . . Biting my lip, I stood up, tied my robe around my tummy (Oh, the sweet growing fertile middle of me!) then closed the door to the bedroom so Dolores wouldn't see me crying and tearing my hair out.

DOLORES

Maybe it be brother Beneficio who keep me up so late last night with his loud friends (all the nopales and beer and chimichangas and papusas are no more) but after I talk to Mrs. Estelle by phone about work then take the bus and walk to Buckwood Estates I no have strength for nothing.

The two dogs bark bark bark so I lock them in the garage then clean the toilet and up the stairs but I get so tired I just get juice from fridge and lay on the plastic bed on porch. There I see the road and security building and can see Dr. Collin come. Shit, if no accident with car last week I just finish and leave whenever and go down the hill to town. But now I must wait and can only think about Dr. Collin. Stop the worry, too much worry!

Instead I look at big yard, everything down lower. I never see no place like this ever. I mean, maybe Governor's Palace in San Salvador, maybe. Swimming, pretty jumping water, horses, sports things, flowers and fruit and trees. Where yard end and where hill begin nobody knows.

Uncle Ilio show me round the city since come from El Salvador last year and now I see things he show me. The Parquat like gold necklace in valley. The orange water shine through Falmouth all the way to smokestacks near me in Circleville. Funny name: Circleville. And big mountains to the right, to . . . to east make the Falmouth glass buildings look small. But who care about this

18

place? No me. Too much hurry and rent rent rent. I miss my country is all I know.

My watch say 2:30. I got job interview at bowling alley later but maybe I forget about that stupid kitchen grease job and go with Uncle Ilio. He tell me over and over about friends in church he likes and wants me come visit where they live. Maybe I go visit new people with God instead of do more stupid work.

I breathe deep. He get home soon—

"Dolores? Hello."

I look up. No! I sleep long. My hair everywhere, titty sticking out.

"Mrs. Estelle left me," I say fast and sit up.

"Whoa, slow down," Dr. Collin say. "I think I surprised you. I didn't mean to interrupt your reverie." He take my shoulders and push me back down on plastic bed. He walk to edge of porch and look at sky and orange flowers in the wood box.

"What time did my wife leave?" he ask.

"When she leave me?"

"Yes—what time was it?"

"Few hours maybe," I say.

"It's a beautiful day, isn't it? Not too hot."

I no answer but quick grab glass I still have on porch with fruit juice.

"How's the house—is it a big mess?"

I smile. "No bad. I clean up the stairs."

He pick dead flowers and throw off porch, then say, "There's still balloons all over the gazebo. When was Estelle's birthday party anyway, a month ago?"

I no answer but just stand and go to glass door to start work again.

"Dolores, wait a second. Don't be in a rush now," the doctor say with nice smile. I stop and right then I know I make big mistake. He walk to the front of me. Jewel eyes look at me. I red in face and look down.

"It's such a pleasure to see you. You look so beautiful. Did you do something with your hair?"

I check work clothes and shake head: No, no, no.

"I'll be the judge of that. Why, your hair just shines . . . and your skin—pure cream, just perfection."

What his words about? "You crazy, Dr. Collin," I said, moving to the door again, face hot.

I go inside and get vacuum and go to living room and keep eye on him all the time. I see him go to kitchen for mail and sit at table and read and forget me. I check watch: 3:45 now. I sleep way too long before so quick work with vacuum and lemon polishing and Windex. After while he leave kitchen and go out front door without words. When he come back he carry big leather box.

"We'll both have to work for awhile, I'm afraid," he say.

"You want eat now? Drink something now?" I ask.

"How nice, how rare, to hear those words. But no, I'm going to take a ride later, so I don't want to fill up. Have you found any treasures today?"

I touch fingers together and they oily from the rag. I stare at him, putting hand on hip.

"I'm looking for a scandal to uncover," he say funny-like. "Have you found any of my wife's sexy lingerie. Perhaps a secret love letter?"

"Always fun, Dr. Collin. No, I no find nothing like that."

"Where are the dogs?" he ask.

"I put in garage. Sorry, I get now."

"No, leave them there. I knew there was some reason it was so quiet. It's wonderful like this, just being alone, without all the usual clamor."

He going to say it and ask it now—I know.

"What are you doing?" he asked.

"Just work hard, that's it."

"Don't worry about the house, Dolores, it looks fine," he say and try to look in my eyes. "I have to talk with an attorney, so I'm going to be down in the lower level."

"I no clean there yet."

"Will you be?"

"Yes, Dr. Collin. I clean it."

"Should I turn on the sauna?" he ask.

There he say it. I know this man.

"Doctor, you my boss—por favor."

He come close to me.

"Dolores, let's try it again. Just like in July."

That stupid afternoon! His woman go to store and I let him move me on the couch.

"You're a sweet Madonna. I just want to eat you up."

He love my cocoa skin and hair down to waist. I know that. There no choice for me. I might lose good job and anyway I lonely woman with nothing and I like to feel good sometime.

"I go to shower," I say. I want to smell wife's lotion and perfume in second drawer of bathroom.

"Yes, perfect, you do what you need to do and I'll get the sauna turned on. Just come down whenever you like."

"OK, Dr. Collin. You win."

SUZANNE

"Kowalski . . . *Kowalski!*"

With one hand gripping the steering wheel, Officer K gave me one of those you-answer-it looks. Even though he was a jerk, I could understand his frustration; he'd been talking with dispatch continuously for the past half-hour.

What a morning! Killings at the Heritage Bank, a series of small robberies, just crazy mayhem all over town. It all would have been business as usual in some Blue Alert in the ghetto on the eastside, but in Falmouth, no way.

Patrolling the quiet streets of the Pinehurst district, we hadn't seen any action yet and I doubted we ever would. Why I'd been assigned to this squad car with this beat cop, out in these suburbs, I'd probably never know, but I had my suspicions. My place was downtown with the stars from SWAT and Investigations, where the specialized action was, but somehow, need it be repeated, female officers never got the choice assignments.

I picked up the mic from the console and pressed for voice.

"No, this is Lieutenant Dunkirk. We're just off Plymouth Boulevard. What's up?"

"There may be some sort of hostage situation on the Concourse," the dispatcher said, her voice grainy as ever.

"You're kidding?"

"Today *kidding* is not a word in my vocabulary."

"Do you need us?"

"No, stay along the canal trail. Be suspicious of anything—anything, hear me? We don't know what this . . . this disturbance is all about."

"Read you loud and clear, kidding aside."

I put the mic back and I glanced over at Kowalski, but couldn't see his eyes through the wrap-around sun glasses. I wondered if he was on edge as much as I was.

"What's the story, Suzie Q?"

Suzie Q! Who is that? For the umpteenth time, I'd just let it pass. I didn't need my personnel file tarnished by this guy's complaints.

"Just keep sniffing the air," I answered.

"No problem with that. Good stench out today."

We turned onto Chenault Drive and blended with the traffic, which was heavier than usual because of the road blocks downtown. We passed a skating rink, the wood skeleton of a new condominium complex, the Wellspring Arts Center, then a mass of purple and orange maples that marked the beginning of Hollydale Park. With everyone no doubt alarmed by the news, the traffic was slow and obedient for a Saturday afternoon.

"I sure would like a smoke," Kowalski said. "Maybe we can stop for dinner early."

This old lifer always wanted a cigarette. I didn't know anybody—well, maybe some of the old dykes who never learned from their prodigal youth—who had that old-fashioned nicotine jones as bad as Kowalski.

"It's gonna be pretty tough to get a break today," I warned, feeling a knawing sense of danger in my gut. It had to be this crime spree sweeping the community, because I couldn't get Ferdinand, my two year-old, off my mind. That cute little *in vitro* turkey baster boy, I just loved him something terrible, not to mention his mother and my forever partner, Sorrelle.

Then from off to our right, traveling against the light, a bicyclist sped across the intersection. A car pulling out slammed on its brakes, then honked. The rider, who was wearing a bright red outfit, pedaled hard, leaning low and aerodynamic over the handlebars.

"That was pretty stupid, and dangerous," I said.

"Sure in a hurry, ain't he?"

I sat up straight. "Yesterday, we'd ignore it, today, let's check it out."

With lights flashing we made a u-turn and headed north up Chenault, then made two quick right turns. Once on Vitae Lane we rolled along slow and invisible, waiting for the rider to appear at the canal trail crossing.

In no time the man sped up to the street, but had to stop because of the congested traffic. He looked quickly left and right, standing over his bike, then checked his wrist watch. Kowalski gave a quick blast with the siren, then accelerated the squad car up to the trail. The rider looked at us, scowling, then took off his sunglasses.

I got out and walked over to him. "Good afternoon," I said. I did some riding myself and admired the bike's raspberry-colored frame, the Shoenberg rims. "You went through a red light one block over," I said with my best authority.

"Did I?" he answered, still breathing hard. "I might not have noticed. I'm completing a timed workout."

A woman pushing her infant in a three-wheel stroller also stopped at the light. "He practically ran us over back there," she said with fire in her eyes. When the light turned green she and her little one continued on their way.

"Where you going in such a hurry?"

"I'm just taking an afternoon ride. I live up in Buckwood." He took a shot of water, then put the bottle back on the center rack.

This is a silly waste of time, I concluded. This guy isn't a danger to anybody. I was tempted to just let him go and get on to more serious business.

"Can I be on my way?" he asked.

23

"No, you can't. I need to see your identification," I said, trying not to sound too apologetic.

Kowalksi came over and stood beside me. Since this was my first stint in the southeast, I needed to be extra vigilant, extra competent, extra tough, or he'd gender fuck me like all the other women on the force.

"You know, I don't have any ID with me," the man explained. "I never carry my license when I go riding."

"No identification, is that what I heard?" my partner grunted, ready to take over.

"Yes—just an anonymous nobody," the rider remarked with a sarcastic smile.

"We'll determine that," Kowalski said in a low, bored voice. He started moving towards the rack over the back tire when a blast of the dispatcher's voice called him back to the squad car.

I followed my partner's lead. "What do you have in your pack?" I asked.

"Come on, are you serious? It's a bunch of junk in there, mostly flat tire paraphernalia."

"I'll have to see what's inside," I said, pulling the hand computer out of the holder on my belt. I punched into the program.

"What's your name?"

"Donald."

"Donald who?"

"Duck."

I stared at him: another asshole Alpha Male.

"If you continue this way, I'll read your rights and—"

"My rights? What rights? I object to this. Just because of your petty—"

"Suzie!" I looked over and Kowalski was waving for me to come. Evidently, the crisis was spreading.

"Wait here. Get your pack ready for inspection. I'll be right back."

He fiddled with the strap on his helmet. "Whatever you say officer, anything to avoid my assignment to the Gulag."

When I got back to the squad car, Kowalski announced, "We have to patrol the bridge into Circleville—pronto."

Good I figured, now I can get back into the thick of things.

"OK, and what about our cyclist here?"

But Officer K was already pointing back to the trail. "You got me," he said.

I turned and saw the man taking off across the intersection. He skipped alongside the bike a few steps, then jumped on. He was running on the red, taking advantage of a brief opening in the traffic.

"Too bad we can't nail him," I said, but not really caring a lick.

"You couldn't catch him anyway, Suzie Q. That trail goes into the Cherry Orchard estates, by the golf course, then up into the hills where there's no access."

I didn't know where in Falmouth he was talking about.

"He's not a piece of this jigsaw anyway," Kowalski continued, turning on the siren and abruptly pulling across the double yellow line. "We got some organized criminals to deal with."

But I thought about the arrogant guy as we headed to the Parquat River, and punched his physical description and what happened into my contacts directory for evening report.

CHRISTINA

We'd been driving so fast for so long that I'd drifted off into a weird space. What had just happened in Falmouth, the noise from the shooting, the yelling, repeated in my mind like a horrible video game. But as the van slowed down I kinda came back to reality and opened my eyes.

I checked out the twins in the back of the van. They were mega-wacked out too, leaning against the big boxes stored back there.

"What's this?" Pribble asked from the driver's seat. He glanced over at Charles riding shotgun. "Should I stop?"

"We should just go, but, hold it, it's an accident or something."

"Go or stop, huh, which one?"

Charles put up his hand abruptly. "Stop then, we'll wait for the others to catch up."

25

The van bounced off onto the shoulder of the road, brakes squeaking right underneath me.

"What's wrong?" Kenny Wayne asked.

"You got me," I answered. "Is Peter crashed?"

"Yea, lucky him."

Charles opened the door and got out and in a minute called Pribble's name.

Pribble slammed the steering wheel and turned the engine off. He said some nasty words and used the Lord's name in vain (he always did that when he knew I was listening) then went outside too. The two of them talked back and forth, then the side doors flew open and Pribble told us, "Get some fresh air if you want."

I crawled out of the van and stood up in the bright sunlight, my legs majorly asleep.

Charles was standing over a man who was lying in the middle of the road. He wore a red get-up (kinda like those fancy Spider Man outfits that all the bikers beamed when they pedaled through Circleville on Saturday mornings). He had one shoe off and was in some prehistoric pain. I immediately felt bad for him. Then—was this for real?—I went into total shock: it was the man who'd guessed the Kenyatta Koffee question that morning, the straight guy who got caught in the twister!

"I tore up my ankle," he complained, biting his lip. "I was trying to cross that ravine over there . . . I was carrying my bike down through some junk and this barrel drum I was stepping on collapsed."

His foot was trashed—even stupid me could see that. When he rolled down his sock his ankle was bulging and purple—gross! I could tell he was embarrassed about being kept down, helpless, in front of everybody, but his foot gave him no choice.

Charles knelt down, shaking his head. "Mister, you're in a bad way," he said.

"Yes, you're absolutely right. Listen, I'm Dr. Collin Merrithew. Are you going into town? I need treatment for this, the quicker the better."

Charles kept quiet. His bald head was sweating and he wiped it with a paper towel. Poor Charles, he'd come down from the mountains early that morning and I could tell he was running on empty.

The doctor wanted someone's attention, and his eyes landed on me. Even though I was kinda scared, I smiled and moved closer, his pain pulling me like a magnet.

"Christina, get back!" Pribble yelled from behind me. I stopped, twirled my eyes and gave him a fahgeettaboutya sneer. He just continued leaning against the van, his thumbs in his pockets, but he sure jumped up straight and did as he was told when Charles ordered, "Brother Pribble, bring the twins!"

After being cooped up in the back for so long, Kenny Wayne and Peter seemed dazed being outside. They were dressed cute in white shirts and black pants cause they'd been the "front men"—whatever that meant—in Falmouth. They walked up to Charles and asked about what was going on.

The doctor pleaded his point-of-view. "Listen, if you take me back, I'd be glad to generously pay you for your efforts. I'm just trying to deal with an unfortunate situation here."

Pribble stepped up and took a closer look at the man. "Forget this, Charles, let's get outta here."

"Please, some patience" Charles said, "especially in this time of need. This man—this man who's a *doctor*—is hurt."

"Man, get real," Pribble pleaded, "Trajan's right behind us, and I ain't going to Resource Hour again tonight, I ain't."

The doctor raised himself up off the asphalt a little bit. His hands were covered with greasy black lines. "Can we stop arguing? How many miles is it to Falmouth?"

"It's quite a ways, you unfortunate soul," Charles said, standing up and stuffing the paper towel in his pocket. "But we do have a special way to help with your problem."

Then I heard something down the highway—Trajan. No way did I want to ride in the jeep next to him. "There's cars coming," I warned everybody, my stomach tightening.

The twins went to work and got the doctor up on his good right foot. Putting his arms over their shoulders, the doctor got carried off the road just before the jeep and the other cars roared by. It was him alright, and he wasn't stopping for nobody. Good.

At the side doors of the van, the twins lowered the doctor down and he sat there rubbing his leg.

"I don't want to get a spasm," he said, kinda inspecting me. "You look very familiar. Do I know you?"

Shoot, I thought, I figured he'd never recognize me in different clothes.

"Yea, the coffee shop."

He nodded his head. "Why, of course: Born to Lose. What are you doing here? You live close by?"

"Circleville," I answered.

Charles put his head out the window, scowling at me. "Christina, please," he said, "we have many miles to go and so much to do." I caught his drift and shut up.

The doctor glanced inside at Charles and Pribble, then read the twins from head to toe.

"Hold your horses now," the doctor said in a loud, strong voice. "Why do I feel like I'm making some terrible mistake?"

Kenny Wayne said, "We're gonna take you with us."

"I can see that's your intention," he answered.

Pribble started the engine.

"Sir, please don't worry," Charles reassured him, wiping the side mirror with his hand. "We can help you, we just can't do it here."

The doctor was still totally suspicious, but he just seemed to give up the fight and scooted inside anyway. The twins crawled in after him and moved back to the treasure of boxes. I got in last and closed the doors, collapsing like a serving of spaghetti.

The doctor and I faced each other as we moved down the highway.

"How do they breath back there?" the doctor asked, looking at the twins.

I just smiled, too tired to say anything.

He stretched his left leg out straight, rubbing his forehead over and over.

"Can you tell me where we're going?" he asked.

"Up into the mountains," I said.

"O.K. But what's in the mountains? I need medical attention, not a weekend getaway."

I held my tongue, knowing that Charles and Pribble were listening in. I offered the doctor the blanket I'd been using earlier, but he waved it off, saying he didn't need it.

Charles turned back from the front seat. "There's a hospital where we're going."

"O.K. But how far away is it?"

"Not far, not far at all. Lean back and rest. You're hurt—you should save your energy."

"What's the name of the hospital, Charles?" the doctor asked.

"I don't know the name of it," he answered, looking back down the highway.

"Hey . . . hey, Charles," the doctor demanded, banging the floor with his hand to get his attention. "Charles!" he repeated, with no response. The doctor tried to raise up and move towards the front seats, but, no, not a good idea.

"They ain't listening," I said in a low voice.

He nodded, pissed, glancing the other way. "Neither are they," he said, pointing at the twins.

"That's Peter, and next to him, against the box, is Kenny Wayne," I said.

"What's your name?"

"Christina."

He stared at me for a second, then his eyes looked right through me and seemed to travel a million miles away. I felt kinda sorry for him cause he was so far away from home, just like us.

"Where'd you put your bike?" I asked, sounding super lame.

"It's still at the dump, with all the other two-thousand dollar pieces of scrap metal," he said in disgust, letting me know from his tone that he didn't want to talk any more.

With Pribble keeping his foot to the floor, the van powered up the highway. Charles read his small pocket Bible, the one he was always writing notes in.

I was morphed out and wanted to sleep in the worst way, but it was impossible on the shaking floor. I couldn't stop my left eye from twitching, so I just shut both eyes and started humming to myself.

I loved to hum. When I hummed it was like a church inside

myself I could go into, a place where I could think about C.W.'s special words. No Onward Christian Doldrums for you, he used to say. I was always proud of being the only one who could remember all his great writings and poems and songs and sayings. I don't know how I did it actually, but all my life I could memorize anything if I really put my mind to it. It just went in one ear and never came out the other. C.W called me his Keeper of the Word. My humming vibrated on the roof of my mouth . . .

> *It's sad that beavers die in the Parquat River*
> *Sad the herons in the wetlands fly fallow*
> *It's sad, though I've never seen a whale*
> *To hear of the whales being driven ashore, the tigers*
> *Run down, though I've never seen a tiger—*
> *But I've got a situation*
> *A human situation*
> *Right here in this town*
> *Right here where promises are broken*
> *And backs are broken*
> *And fists turn soft as pudding*
> *Right here on this street*
> *Where children howl in glee at colored pictures*
> *Lured by the Chameleon*
> *You know, the sneaky Chameleon*
> *That keeps us all poor and sick—*

. . . Bumps in the highway made my head dip and brought me back from the song. The van slowed waaay down and I could tell we were starting the steep curvy grind up into the mountains. I was stoked to see the island again and wondered if anything had changed.

"I need an ice pack in the worst way," the doctor groaned, pressing his leg and ankle. "I think it's the tarsus bone."

"Yea, it looked nasty, that's for sure," I said. "Do you ride your bike a lot?" I asked, embarrassed that I was still making silly sports talk. But, hey, what do you say to a doctor if you're not in his office, sick?

30

"Sure, about forty miles a week," he said.

I thought about the two bikes Trajan's men had dumped in the bushes on the side of the little road that led to the cable. Nobody knew who'd dragged em up from the valley, or, knowing what kind of place Plentiful was, why they had in the first place. But they were awesome bikes with pretty red and silver stripes.

"What about you?" the doctor asked.

Oh, my God, I asked myself, is he asking me for the skinny? I waited, half-expecting Pribble or Charles' objections, but nothing, so I went for it.

"I used to ride my bike to school a long time ago, but I don't ride now—bike's cost too much."

"Buy a used one," the doctor suggested.

I looked into the shadows, trying my best to find the doctor's face, his eyes, but it was getting too dark to focus. The doctor musta lost focus too cause he didn't ask me any more questions. Bouncing back and forth on the vibrating floor, I kept switching my mind from this to that to avoid thinking about Falmouth. As we got higher into the mountains it got colder and colder. I was going to use the blanket for warmth so I could take a little nap before our arrival, but then I slammed myself for being selfish. I did right and offered it again to the doctor, who took it this time. Every day I tried to give up something I had or deserved or wanted so that somebody else could benefit; it just made me feel better inside.

After a long time, maybe one or two hours, the van slowed down and stopped.

Charles turned back to us. "Quiet now!" he demanded under his breathe. "Think about your actions."

SHAWNTE

The whole posse was hours late getting to the mountains. I probably should have expected it, what with all the shit that'd been happening since we started making moves above ground, but still, a plan is a plan and the plan was four o'clock sharp. And now here I was, cold as ice, hangin out in the trees like a vampire, listening to the same excuses from the same old mouths.

That's what was different about Trajan: when he spit something ill, things happened. I'd noticed that about him way back when I still had my job cooking at Olympic Ribs and Pies, when he would come in and eat on Thursday nights, then later when we worked at the Silver Lining Co-Op together. The man followed through on what he said, period. So, when he promised that some real food would be coming to Plentiful, I believed the man and lined up behind him.

Then someone finally said the magic words, "They're here!" and, yea, the cars and trucks started pulling in, lights off, tires munching the ground.

The ten of us who'd been waiting moved out under the open stars. I rubbed my hands and arms for warmth and tried to spy my man and, yea, there he was, his bad tall self getting outta the jeep. Hm, hm, hm, I thought, if only I'd met Trajan before rehab and getting saved, I woulda been tempted to let him blow out my back in a fine tailbone tribute our very first night together. But, not living in the past, I buried those thoughts and hurried over and hung by his side, thanking the Lord for the moonlight that let us see beyond our noses.

Trajan started picking people out and I stepped in front to get chosen.

"Can you lift?" he asked me.

"Shoot, can 50 Cent bark in the woods. Sure I can lift," I answered, so he took me and four other brethren over to the van. The identical twins were opening the back door with Little Miss Sweetheart, and there was another man sitting there who I didn't recognize. As we walked up, the stranger asked nobody in particular, "Where are we?"

I was closest to him, so I spoke up, "In the Browns, mister."

"Really? It's cold," he said.

"Yea, you got that right. Wait til the morning hours."

"Is there a town nearby?"

"Couldn't tell you that," I answered, figuring he was a new recruit from Circleville.

All the island people were quick and quiet as mice moving the stuff that had been gathered from the trip back home. There'd better be some food in those boxes or there's gonna be hell to pay in the coming days.

The stranger inched outta the van and tried to stand up, but—ouch!—he just moaned low, favoring his left foot.

"Hey, Christina, my friend, it looks like I'll need some help again," the man complained.

Christina put a box in Peter's arms then hurried over to the man's side. So, I calculated, this was Trajan's thump thump. Even though I'd been around for a while, I was still trying to get the Plentiful blueprint down pat, and it was good to place this young bitch on the right square. But look at her, skinny as can be, right in the middle of where I wanna go.

"Hi Shawnte," Peter said, walking by.

"Hey, what's up?" I said as he faded outta sight.

Trajan had been talking about recruiting Peter into the Security Circle; he said he liked how disciplined and obedient he was. The other look-a-like, Kenny Wayne, wasn't ever mentioned: probably too tight with C.W.

Trajan finally walked up to all of us, with Charles, the good man of the cloth, hanging on his belt.

"Who are you?" he asked the new recruit.

"I'm Dr. Collin Merrithew."

"You a real doctor, or just a book doctor?"

"I'm a medical doctor."

"You hurt?"

"Yes, I am. I think I have some ligament damage and a broken bone, and I need a soft cast put on my foot and lower leg."

Trajan didn't pay him any mind, and just told all the lifters to go move the two large boxes in the back of the van, but to be careful cause they were backbreakers and special cargo. And, sure nuff, Trajan was right because it took all my booty—and I'm a big strong woman—to help move what I hoped was a load of groceries. As we went about our business, I kept looking back at the van. Trajan and the newcomer were still yapping at each other, and by the time we finished and walked back, the stranger was getting hot under the collar.

"Listen, I don't know what kind of covert operation you have going here, but I don't want any part of it. Charles said you had a hospital. That hardly seems possible so … "

A man ran up to Trajan and whispered in his ear.

"Doc, we gotta go," Trajan said. "You ready?"

"Are you crazy? I'm not going anywhere!" he said. "I want a ride back."

"Back?"

"Yes, back—back to Falmouth, where I live."

But Trajan scolded him, "I live down the mountain too, we all do. We all wanna sleep in our own beds."

"Well, you're not injured."

"Yea, well, we're hurtin pretty good, it's not just you."

The doctor looked away, frustrated, then started talking back: "This is just—I don't know what to say. It's very simple, just make a call and leave me by the side of the road. I'll pay for a helicopter to come up from the valley. Come on, I have a surgical practice, people who need me."

"Merrithew?"

"Yes."

"*We* need a doctor."

"What? Repeat that again."

"You're the doctor we need—you! You're him."

The doctor slapped his thigh hard and stood up as best he could from the side of the van.

"What kind of mumbo jumbo is that?" he asked, then, like a crazy mutha fucka, the man went after Trajan! He wasn't a big guy, but he was filled with fear strength, and it took a sec for Trajan to pin him against the van, while I held his arms down. My face was close to Trajan's, and he couldn't help but notice how quickly I jumped to protect his ass.

"OK, OK, stop it!" the medicine man yelled out, his body giving up. Trajan and I let go and the guy slumped down, breathing hard.

Trajan slapped his shoulder. "Don't worry, Doc. We'll get you taken care of. I bet you're used to always getting your way, huh? Well, this time we got the infantry, and like C.W. says, "The hand of privilege can only reach so far.""

"Listen, I've had a very . . ." He stopped to catch his breath, then continued: "I've had a very, very long day and I'm not going anywhere. You've got the wrong doctor."

This hit Trajan's last nerve. He stepped up and with a move that woulda made my homies proud, he grabbed the man by the hair, straightened him up, and kicked him right in his bad leg. The poor doctor let out a yell to raise the dead, then fell over. Jesus Almighty, I thought, that beef is squashed! Trajan waved at us, "Put him in the jeep—drag him if you have to." So, without any more friction, we got the wounded dude moved over and put in the back seat, with Charles next to him. Trajan told me to get in the back too, and I had to secretly smile at my good luck. When I got situated there was a rap on the window. It was the girl. I rolled the window down and she said, "Here," dropping a blanket in my lap, "it's the doctor's." Hoping Trajan wouldn't notice, I just handed the man the blanket without a word, and he put it across his lap real snug. I looked back up, but the girl was gone.

Trajan got in the front passenger seat and the driver started the engine. Real quick Trajan reached back and put something in my hand. I checked it: Alright, a bag of peanuts—that'll taste damn good! Outside, all the other vehicles started up too, roaring like lions, then we all pulled out and made a caravan with no headlights up the mountain road.

"You ever been in the Brown Mountains before, Doc?" Trajan asked cheerfully, like he had a new job as a tour guide. The doctor was silent as a stone and I could feel his body shaking next to me. Trajan just laughed. "What happened with the generator, Pribble?" he asked the driver.

"Which one you talkin about?" he asked back, his fingers tapping the steering wheel.

"*I'm* not stupid. Are *you* stupid? Which one you think I'm talkin about?

"OK, OK, I know. I guess there was some guy from the Peaks, names Bosco, that knows heavy equipment and got it up an going. It blew once or twice, but they fixed it. That's all I know."

'That's all I needed to know. Charles, what about gas?"

Charles leaned forward. "About fifteen gallons, Trajan." He sat back in his seat. "I pray that everything will go according to plan, like C.W. said."

Trajan looked out the window. "Well, so far, ain't nothin going according to his plan, is it? But that's alright, the worse it is now, the sweeter the victory parade in Circleville."

Then Trajan snapped his fingers at Pribble, pointing left as the road split. We bounced along, the trees closing in around us, then we came to the same dirt field where the cable had dropped us off earlier in the day. Trajan told Pribble to pull far left and let the others pull in behind us. One by one, all the drivers got out and walked over to the jeep, looking like ghosts from a horror film the way they appeared outta the dark. Trajan got out to address the group.

Sitting, watching, the medicine man asked Charles, "What are we doing . . . and what is that thing over there?"

"Just wait, we'll all be going across the canyon. It'll just take a few minutes," Charles answered. "Would you like to say a prayer with me, Dr. Merrithew?"

"No need to ask, Charles, that's not—I'm not a religious man."

"Well, you gonna be real soon," Pribble said, glancing in the rear view mirror, acting like he was trying to make his mark in the game. The medicine man just ignored the comment.

Trajan stuck his head back inside. "Doc, you gonna be pullin your shenanigans, or can we treat you—"

"Just shut up. I'm your prisoner—I don't need the condition of my foot set back any more than it already has been."

"Whatever floats your boat, Doc. But all of you, get out and go over by the stairs."

We did as the boss man said. The medicine man kept the blanket wrapped around his shoulders (he had to be cold, being dressed like he was about to hike a Stairmaster) and crawled along with the twins help. I stayed close behind, getting a little nervous about going over the canyon again.

There musta been thirty people hanging at the power building when we walked up. I'd already been over the cable twice, but it still gave me goosebumps seeing it stretched into the darkness, disappearing out where I knew Plentiful was located. Since all the windows were covered up island-side, you couldn't see any light coming from over there, only the points of the mountains rising up a long ways off.

Trajan got up on the platform to speak. The long metal room—C.W. called it our alpine gondola—was hanging from the cable, and off to the left was the power building where the cable turned round two huge metal wheels. You could hear the machinery roaring, the cable hummin like an electric amplifier.

"Women go first," Trajan ordered, "then anyone helping our new guest. But you have to hurry cause we still got supplies to bring over."

One by one, the women came outta the crowd and walked up the steps to the gondola. The medicine man made it too, one slow step at a time. When the doors slid open we got inside, careful with the slippery metal floor.

"Doc?" Trajan said, standing outside on the platform. "The guardians will never leave you from here on out, got that? I'll see you on the other side, then you can meet our leader." Trajan slammed the metal door shut and slapped the side for good luck.

My stomach started turning flips and my palms got clammy as the gondola swung free as a bird under our feet. The medicine man stared as the view changed from earth to open air. He didn't seem afraid as we floated along like a planet in outer space, just thinking hard, then harder still. I kept looking at people's faces to feel secure, making sure I didn't look down into the canyon.

"This place we're going to, what is it?" the doctor asked anyone.

"It's part of an old mine," Kenny Wayne said.

"Where?"

"You can't see it yet."

A woman in the far corner chimed in, "Do you know the Byzantium Metal Works in Circleville? Well, this was one of their mines. Iron ore or something. Closed up about ten years ago, way before Byzantium moved overseas. My Daddy, he worked up here a couple summers. None of us knew where he was going to, but he'd leave on Saturday and come back two weeks later on a Saturday. I remember his pack would be filled with pine cones for Mommy and us kids."

"Never heard of it," the doctor said. "Is this the only way of getting across?"

"I figure," Kenny Wayne said.

"That doesn't make sense. How could they get any minerals out of here?" The doctor pressed his face against the window, examining, analyzing, then he looked my way for the 411.

"Don't ask me, I dunno," I filled in before he could say another word.

Then a voice—"There it is!"—grabbed our attention, and out of the blackness you could start to see some tree tops, smokestacks, and roofs of buildings.

Trajan's squeeze started singing a song, which was a tradition whenever people arrived in Plentiful. I never really joined the singing, but just pretended I knew the words. Black folks are always supposed to be into music, and I didn't want anything to do with that old reflex. This was supposed to be a new place, with new ideas.

As always, the ditty was outta C.W.'s songbook:

Circleville
Proud lady with a river companion
Mother of all cities
Keeper of the homeless on the streets
The shadows in the parks
The ragged by the riverside
Your arms comfort the blessed children
Whose hopes grow tall behind warm windows.
Circleville
Proud lady with a river companion.
Mother of all cities
You will sow the first seed.

Listening, I had to hand it to the little bitch (C.W. always called her the Lord's little diva), she wasn't no Beyonce or Missy, but she did have a songbird's voice. Then the other women, who no doubt knew the song from the sunrise Morning Glory meetings, joined in too, and I have to admit, the ditty put a glow in my heart.

Then Plentiful came at us right outta the night. As we hit land and slid up to the loading dock, people be running up and waving at us, lookin hungry as a horde of mosquitos.

When the gondola stopped and the door flew open, I couldn't praise the Lord enough for the safe journey.

✦ ✦ RUTH ✦ ✦

"...And dear Lord, Jesus Christ, protect our flock. Our health is our wealth and we need food and medicine to protect us during the coming winter. My old bones feel a new season in the air, so please, if we prove worthy of your infinite kindness, start a fire to keep us warm here in this wilderness and provide bread for our tables—"

Somebody opened the bedroom door.

"Ruth, you in there?" a voice inquired. "Ruth? Ruth?"

I must go now, sweet Shepherd. Please watch over us and heed my words. Amen.

"Hello? Who are you?" I asked the mystery person from my spot on the floor.

The door shut without a word. I put my hands on the chair and raised up slowly off my knees, then shuffled out into the living room. Outside, dark figures were running up the street. Was somebody pulling a prank, I wondered, or was there business to attend to at the main building? I returned to the back bedroom and tidied up the makeshift bed I'd created for myself.

I loved this little old house. It reminded me of the blue two-bedroom that Walter and I lived in when he was working the river docks, before the City Council made way for the Sloat Business Park. A rumor had gotten out that the place was infested with rats, which wasn't true, but I let the others think it was because it gave me some peace and quiet and solitude. But now ... well, I was afraid my sanctuary had been discovered.

The mountain air made my spine hurt something terrible,

so I bundled up as best I could, wrapping a towel I'd found in the kitchen around my neck, then buttoning up my coat good and tight. Yes, despite predictions to the contrary, this old lady was ready to start preparing dinner! Snuffing the candle, I stepped outside—the chilly autumn air passed right through me—and joined the others heading up to the main building. I wondered if they'd recruited more mouths to feed.

When I entered through the side doors, the tall ceiling echoed with the voices of the scores and scores of C.W.'s followers who were using this immense place as home. There were strict rules limiting the light that could be used at night, but there was no holding back all the loud sounds from the congregation.

To keep from getting jostled too much by all the youngsters, I slipped behind the makeshift curtain that blocked the kitchen from the rest of the community living area. Not many people went behind the curtain because it meant you were volunteering for work, and to most of these religious renegades work was equal to prison time.

I stepped carefully through what meager foodstuffs remained for meals, being extra careful about any wet spots. Then, lo and behold, underneath a pile of plastic bottles, I found a forgotten (or hidden) bag of Wonder Wraps. Thank you, Lord, I said in praise, thank you. I quickly stuffed the food in my coat pocket, then made my way along the back wall over to the tall metal-framed doors that looked out towards the loading dock.

The doorway was filled with youngsters from the Riverside and the Peaks, all dressed in blue jeans and gray sweatshirts. At my age I could never create a space for myself in a crowd, so I had to find a safe spot behind someone and go with the human flow. But I bumped into the man ahead of me a couple times and he glanced back.

"Hey, Ruth. I didn't know it was you." It was one of those sweet twins, Kenny Wayne. He was pushing a wheelchair, of all things.

"Don't mind me," I apologized. "Where are you going with that contraption?"

But before he could answer, he forged ahead through the

crowd, and luckily I was able to follow behind as he moved over to the steps of the loading dock. His twin, Peter, pretty Christina, and Shawntee, a black woman from the kitchen, were standing with a man I didn't recognize.

"Sorry, Dr. Merrithew, but this is all we got," Kenny Wayne said, placing the wheelchair in front of the stranger. The man shook his head, smirking.

"Where did you find that old thing? It looks like an antique from a state hospital," he complained, dropping down into the chair anyway. He was disabled or hurt or something, I couldn't tell for certain. "Still, that's much better," he added.

Did Kenny Wayne say, doctor? A real doctor? I certainly didn't remember the man from any clinic in Circleville. If it was true, how wonderful!

Christina stepped up and tucked the blanket in behind his back, and I realized I had to make myself useful in some way. "You must be hungry," I said, stepping in front of the seated man.

He looked at me closely. "Who are you?" he asked suspiciously.

"That's Ruth," Kenny Wayne answered before I could speak.

I pulled the food out from under my coat. I knew the others were hungry and would be watching my hands closely.

"Here, try this," I said, handing him the little cellophane roll. "It's our original dish from the kitchen," I said proudly, watching the doctor unwrap it and start eating. "It's called a Wonder Wrap. Rice with soybeans in the center and just a bit of catsup. Shawnte helped cook it."

"It's dry and tasteless," the doctor said, chewing quickly, nodding his head, "but I'm ravenous."

"It's good for you," I said, handing him two more just to be generous.

"You know, I don't think I'll be able to eat these—here, take them," he said, holding the packets up. But before I could accept the food back, Shawntee reached out and grabbed it from the doctor's hand.

"There's going to be a serving later," I said, scowling at the young lady. Where did she learn her manners anyway?

"Women supposed to be fed first, so I'm just gettin my due, that's all," she said, turning away and disappearing into the crowd. I knew Shawnte from the kitchen; she certainly had a mind of her own, and most certainly got her due when it came to food.

Then a voice rang out, "Here comes another load," and we all watched as the gondola appeared out of the darkness like a train out of a tunnel. It slowed down then slowed some more, the motor in the engine room growling low, the gondola finally clanging into place at the loading dock, swinging to and fro. How they got that old thing running I'd never know.

A hundred voices murmured and surged towards the platform as the sliding doors opened. I noticed Christina didn't respond much, but just stood there. The poor dear seemed dazed and exhausted, a child in adult clothing and also, I was afraid, pretending adult ways. Up on the platform, Preacher Charles stepped out, followed by Trajan, Pribble and some others.

Charles immediately raised his hands in greeting. "Thank you for the homecoming and God bless all of you, but will everyone please move back so we have room to disembark and unload the supplies. And there's too much light shining from inside the building. It's dangerous. Please go back inside. Please, I beg you."

Trajan fixed his eyes on our group as he walked down the steps, then pushed his way towards us through the crowd. When he got to us he grabbed the grips of the wheelchair from Kenny Wayne. "This way," he said, pushing the doctor away from the main entrance. Christina, Pribble, and the twins followed Trajan and the doctor as they passed around the corner of the building. I decided to nip at their heels and set off walking, careful not to trip over the tree roots crossing the path. I wanted to know what this doctor was up to.

We passed the two out-buildings where the storage rooms were located, then moved down to that short dead-end street with the cracked asphalt surface that everyone facetiously called The Boardwalk. There were three houses on the south side of the street, and two on the north, one the little gingerbread-decorated abode I'd been using as my sanctuary. Charles told me they were the original homes of the company bosses at the mine. Because every-

one was up at the cable, the houses were dark and deserted, looking as abandoned as they did when we first inhabited the island
eighteen days before.

Stopping at the gate in front of my little house, Trajan motioned for Kenny Wayne to take over the wheelchair.

"This is where you're gonna to be staying, Doc," he said.

"Great. I couldn't be more delighted," the man said sarcastically. "Reminds me of Princeton and summer trips to the Adiron-
dacks."

"Well, I wouldn't know nothin about that, but it's gonna have
to do, that's all there is to it."

"Is there a refrigerator in there?"

"We don't have much electricity," Pribble added.

"No ice?"

"Possibly we do," Trajan said.

"What's that mean?" the doctor asked.

"It depends on you, Merrithew," Trajan said, bending down
close to the man's face. "See, the only reason you're here—the only
reason—is because of what you know. All them big medicine facts
in your brain—you use that info right, you might get some ice,
you don't, you get nothin."

Pribble giggled. "That's right, Doc—"

"Clam up!" Trajan spit at Pribble, who promptly looked down
at the ground.

Trajan stepped away from the doctor and put his boot against
the old white picket fence at the gate. The fence leaned as if it was
about to collapse. Trajan was a clumsy brute without an ounce of
Christian love and compassion in his heart, and I pleaded to myself,
Oh, don't knock that down. Taking matters into my own hands, I
stepped up out of the shadows and started being neighborly.

"I know this house," I chimed in, walking up to the gate. "I
think it might even be older than yours truly."

"What do you want, grandma?" Trajan asked. Much to my
relief, he put his foot down.

"Nothing important really. My name's Ruth. I thought I
might help if I could. I've been staying in that house."

"In this place?"

"Yes."

Trajan stepped away from the group and motioned to me. "Get over here," he demanded.

He started walking with me back towards the main building.

"How is it inside?"

"There's no rodents, if that's what you mean."

"You sure?"

"Yes, I'm sure. I sleep there."

"I just heard stories, that's all. Listen, get some ice or something for the doctor, hear?"

"I'd be glad to, Trajan. Where's the man from, is he local?"

"Don't ask, just keep your eye on him."

"Of course, Trajan. I'll try to help him. Does C.W. know about—"

"What did I just say? Just keep the doctor in one piece, get it?"

"Me, an old lady, caring for the doctor? OK, if that's my mission, fine, but I'll tell you right now, there's not much for his ankle. I'll see what I can dig up from what they brought back from Falmouth."

"Good. You be my senior citizen helper from now on."

"Sure, dear, if you're a gentleman about it."

But since Trajan had already turned back to the others, I knew my request had fallen on deaf ears.

CHRISTINA

I felt stoked to be back on the island. I was like a real mountain girl now, off the city streets, just running around, grooving, touching the trees. Circleville would always be my home, but I was kinda amazed at how it was starting to feel more and more like history all the time.

Since I was tall for my age and took big steps, I always walked faster than everyone else, so now I was waaaay ahead of everybody on the trail we were taking down to C.W.'s headquarters. I stopped

and waited for them to catch up, slapping my thighs restlessly. I started thinking about Spooky and Miss Cheesecake and realized Plentiful had no dogs or cats, not a one, just squirrels and jays. Looking up,
I thought: Hello there, twinkle twinkle, twinkling stars, it's me, I'm
back. And trees, I can hear you whispering about me, so don't think
I don't know what you're feeling under your bark.

It seemed like I was waiting forever for them to appear on
the trail and come down through the rocks and catch up with
me. Waiting; waiting; and waiting some more. OK, hurry up now,
I whispered. Come on, somebody say my name. Kenny Wayne?
Anybody—please. But there wasn't anyone there to say hello, to
protect me from my mind that was starting to run faster and faster.
There was no stopping it . . . *You ugly stinky breath face . . . stiff finger
you . . . stop it! stop it now! Don't try . . . broken buttons spilling . . . rough
lips weird smile above me . . . ah! ah! ah! ah! . . . just watch me don't
touch . . . just watch me turn slow spreading . . . weird stinky breathe man
. . . stop it stiff finger . . . stop*—I started spinning around in circles
to free my brain, then did some jumping jacks, then just stood still
and breathed deep for a minute to calm down.

Jeez, I want to see C.W. sooo bad! His place by the cliffs was
a secret that only a few of us from Pope Street knew about. I was
sure of that, cause when I went into the main building I could
tell from what people said that nobody had any idea where C.W.
stayed. And I knew I was the youngest who'd been there, so that
was pretty cool too.

C.W., he just wanted to be alone most of the time. The only
people he wanted around were people he could trust, or somebody
who could do something important for him. But he liked having
friends from the old neighborhood around the most. All the other new people who had joined up after the fire and riots treated
him different, like he was a big celebrity or something. I mean,
the twins and I were cousins, Trajan was the brother of C.W.'s best
friend, and Charles had been the pastor at the Inner City Path of
Peace Church, so we all went way back together, and we loved and
respected C.W., but we didn't worship him.

I thought about *The Golden Stories* and *The Melopedia* that
C.W. had written; what was the next part of that song about The

Chameleon that I got halfway through in the van? Then I heard footsteps, and finally there were people up the trail.

They all moved slow cause of the doctor, and when they passed by, talking, they didn't even notice me in the shadows, which I kinda liked. Call me Invisible Girl; the blotto fourteen year-old no one can see. I kept quiet and followed behind em, ears pealed for info, keeping a special eye on the doctor.

When we came up to the building by the cliffs, two young guardians with rifles stopped us. Just the sight of those rifles sent a chill down my neck. They patted us down and led us over to the patio in front of the headquarter doors. Trajan and Charles talked for a sec, then disappeared inside.

Maybe it was my imagination, but the air from the canyon seemed to rise up extra chilly. I hugged myself to stay warm. The moon was rising and I wanted to say out loud, Look at the happy white moon make the mountains glow, but I thought I would sound goofy, so I just kept my mouth shut.

"Is that what we crossed on that tram?" the doctor asked, pointing down into the canyon.

"Yea, scary ain't it," Pribble said. "We're all alone." But just then, Charles opened the front door of the headquarters. "Pribble, please come in now," he said.

Pribble scratched the back of his neck, his smile going totally south. Knowing he had no other choice, he followed Charles inside. After a few minutes I was called too, and as I passed through the doors I turned back and waved good-bye to Kenny Wayne and the doctor.

The headquarters had definitely gone through some genetic changes since my last visit. There were two camping lanterns lighting up the room now, and on the floor against the back wall was a big mattress with two other guardians standing by. C.W. was sitting in a chair on a small rug in the middle of the room, next to a corny little table with books and a vase with flowers and a glass of water on it. Pribble was standing off to the side, looking majorly bummed, and Trajan and Charles were back in the corner arguing.

As I walked up, C.W. took a long drink then set the glass down and smacked his lips. "Christina!" he declared in his funny, squeeky voice. "Come here, Golden Throat. Tell me the good news." It seemed like I'd heard his voice my whole life, like at demonstrations downtown, on the TV and radio, during the poetry marathons, hanging out at the Silver Lining Co-Op, even at Wednesday night house meetings. His voice was always waking people up, always making people laugh and think, and now, here at Plentiful, I felt warm inside hearing it again.

"Hi, C.W." I said.

"Hello sweetheart, how was work?"

"Same old same old—just cups of coffee. But I got something for you."

I pulled out the wad of money from my pocket, holding it in both hands and offering it.

"Wow, you've been putting in some overtime. Thank you. You can just set it there on the table," C.W. said.

I put the bills by the vase then stepped back in front of him.

"Well, what are you waiting for, tell me everything. Did you see any of Circleville?"

I let out a nervous laugh. "Little bits, that's all. We were moving pretty fast."

"The maples should be changing along the river, huh?"

"Yea, I guess, I didn't really—"

"Did you come straight up to the mountains?"

Jeez, Louise, what were these speed freak questions!

"No, we went and did stuff."

"I'm curious, why'd you do that?"

"After Trajan picked me up on 17th, he said we had to run some errands. I knew we were in a hurry, but . . . he said not to worry about it."

"That's a lie," Trajan yelled from the shadows along the wall.

C.W. chuckled, his fat tummy bouncing, then he started fiddling with the buttons on his shirt, which didn't seem to be lined up right. As long as I'd known C.W., he never seemed to know how to wear clothes. He always looked like he'd just pulled everything out of the hamper, and no matter how much we teased him about his zipper being down or not wearing any socks or his shirt being torn, he could never get his act together. He looked Trajan's way: "Trajan please, it's a little too late in the day for harsh language. We can talk later."

"You're right, we will," he said, like he was challenging C.W.

C.W. looked at me again, smiling like he was my good friend, checking my eyes closely. "Well, how about it? You ready?" he asked playfully.

"Ready for what?"

"What do you think?"

"*The Melopedia?* Right now?" He has got to be kidding!

"Sure, why not. Everybody's here, but that's OK, isn't it?"

"OK," I said, kicking my mind into gear. "Go for it—choose."

"Alright, let's see, how about an old one like "Swen Bickert". No problem. Standing up straight, I began reciting the words:

> *Swen Bickert, Swen Bickert, he tapped the soles*
> *of people's shoes*
> *Swen Bickert, the great shoemaker, played the kazoo*
> *He played the kazoo*
> *Working at his shop on Creighton Street*
> *Hello, what's doing? He'd say to the people he'd*
> *Be so sweet in his first reply*
> *He'd be so sweet in his first reply*
> *Swen Bickert, Swen Bickert, blind as the buffers he used to shine*
> *The leather upon your feet—*

C.W. raised his arms for me to stop, laughing. I caught my breath. "C.W., what are you doing? I'm not finished."

"OK, OK, wait now, what about "True Religion"? Give that a shot."

That one was easy. I'd repeated that a zillion times.

> *Religion ain't nothin but your glorious eyes*
> *Wise with love at the pink day breaking.*
> *Religion ain't nothin but your soft white breasts*
> *The relish of life for the baby who takes it—*

"God Almighty, Christina," he interrupted again, "now I remember your powers of recollection, little lady."

I didn't know what his problem was, but interrupting a poem or a song had always been very uncool and off limits.

"I'm gonna get you on this one, because I'm sure nobody here, not Charles or Trajan or anybody, will remember it. What about "Archangel Michael"?

"I like that one, it's neat," I said, breathing deep, concentrating . . .

Am I crazy
Or did Archangel Michael just float down the middle of the street?
And if you listen real close
Near the Path of Peace Church
Isn't that his horn pleading beep beep beep.
I'm sick, he pleaded, for so long
Please take me to Emergency
I can't go on.
Am I wrong
Or did Michael not die for the sins
Of the City Fathers?
Who chewed on numbers
And filled their coffers
Making sucking sounds down the hospital corridors.
Lights out, they ordered
And the sick disappeared across
The night border—

I was going to dive into the third verse, but I could tell C.W. was already in hyper-mode thinking about something else, so I just stopped, frustrated.

"Christina, thank you, that was priceless. I'm so honored."

I smiled, feeling better than I had all day, but still kinda angry with him. I knew he knew I was tired and wanted to be dismissed, but his eyes still hung on me.

"Listen, before you test my friendly mattress, tell me about what happened down below. Just give me a thumbnail sketch. And don't worry about Trajan, he'll give me his version later."

The whole room seemed to zone in on me.

"I don't know, C.W. What you asking me for? What do you

want me to say, everybody was robbing places and taking stuff?"

"Well, sure, if that's the truth. But some people got hurt, didn't they?"

I took a sec and got my courage up. "Well, I don't know about anybody getting hurt, but . . . yea, it got all ber–serk and there was shooting." I purposely didn't go on.

"Who were you with?"

"I changed around. They picked me up in the van, then I changed to the car, then back to the van again for the trip up here."

"Did you go to the bank?"

I didn't want to say it, but that was the first place Trajan took me. There were other True Believers in cars in the bank parking lot, and Trajan got together with two of the men. He told everybody to get down and stay down, then those three left and a minute later everything went ballistic with guns and terrible voices. Trajan came rushing back and yelled for everyone to split fast. He said he'd meet us back at the abandoned Pillsbury dairy just north of Circleville, and he did show up a while later, by himself. That's when he gave Charles the van, and Pribble, the twins, and me jumped in and left town. But, just then, facing C.W., I just kept quiet about it all, like I was in another universe.

"OK, I can see this is a loaded subject and will go nowhere," C.W. said. He raised his fist to his lips and gave a little belch, staring into space, then turned to me again. He was trying to be smooth and in control, but I knew him too well and could see he was working on some major damage control.

"There were casualties in Falmouth," he said carefully. "Two men died. Two men died and it's important you don't tell anyone outside of this room about it, OK?" My mind fixed on the two men who had gone with Trajan at the bank.

"Is that understood, Christina?" C.W. repeated.

"Sure, my lips are zipped," I agreed.

"We'll honor them tomorrow. They're heroes and share our roots. But going to the bank was just asking to be fed to the lions. That violence was our mistake, and now all we can do is atone for it." C.W. took another drink of water, then wiped his mouth.

50

"Do I look as tired as you?" he asked me, breaking into a grin.

"You don't look tired, C.W." I answered.

"Good, because I don't feel tired. I'm just getting warmed up. I've got fresh legs and a clear mind and I'm ready for a full fifteen rounds. Christina, I'm sorry about what happened, now go on over and lie down."

"Do you have any new songs?" I asked real quick before walking away.

"I've got a couple Mozart melodies developing, but rest first."

"OK, but am I going to be singing at Resource Hour?"

"Sure, special diva, who else?"

Happy to hear that, I went over and layed down on the mattress, curling my long legs up like a leopard. Maybe it was my imagination, but it seemed like Trajan was staring at me from across the room. Resting my head on my hands, I just wanted to sleep forever in this warm, safe spot.

"OK, let's meet our next contestant," C.W. announced.

Charles walked outside and came back with the doctor, who pushed himself along in the wheel chair, followed by Kenny Wayne. He rolled up and stopped in front of C.W.

"Well, I understand we have a doctor in the house," C.W. said.

"Please," the doctor quickly responded, "this isn't a spaghetti western."

"So you liked those old movies too, huh?"

The doctor just looked at C.W. real serious-like.

"We're blessed by your presence, Dr. Meredith."

"Merrithew," the doctor complained, folding his hands in his lap. "If nothing more, my name is Merrithew."

C.W. smiled, rubbing his stomach. "Yes, well excuse me, my sources got it wrong. That does happen occasionally in my position." He reached over to take another drink of water.

"What's your name?" the doctor asked.

"Me? Charlton Wayne Jokelson. Everybody calls me C.W."

"Mr. Jokelson, if you can bestow happiness on all the inhabitants here, could you bestow some on me. My foot's severely injured and I need medical attention in Falmouth as soon—"

"Wait, wait, wait," C.W. interrupted, "you're getting too complicated for me."

"Not at all. I need to go back to Falmouth where I can have an x-ray and likely have my leg put in a cast. It's that simple."

"I sympathize with you, Dr. Merrithew, I do, but we have an infirmary. It isn't a full hospital yet, although that's something we would like to ultimately develop. We'll take you there immediately and do whatever you request. Is that all right?"

"Don't be ridiculous—"

C.W. raised his hand up. "Dr. Merrithew, I'm sorry, but I need to stop you. Give me a moment with the others first, then we can continue. What you're saying is very important." C.W. sat up in his chair and looked around the room, "Come to me everyone. But not you Christina." The guardians, Charles, Kenny Wayne, Pribble, and Trajan obediently moved over and stood in front of C.W.

C.W. started in, "Despite all the problems, today was a great success. I haven't talked with everyone yet, but from all reports we did what we had to do; we confronted the Chameleon and proved we can stand our ground. So, let the Devil take a bite out of us, justice will still prevail, and here on this mountaintop our kingdom will be established, that's God's will.

Charles, talk to everyone in the main building. Announce that Resource Hour is canceled. Tell everyone to rest and be happy because tomorrow is going to be an important day. But now I want everyone to leave because I have to talk with the doctor. Christina and Kenny Wayne, you can stay and go back later if you want."

So Charles and Pribble and Trajan split. As their voices disappeared up the trail, C.W. hunched over in that my-back-is-hurting-so-bad position. Even though I was totally wiped out and kinda embarrassed cause the doctor was watching, I still got up and went over to give him a massage.

"Thank you, Christina. Are you thinking good thoughts?"

"Trying to," I said. C.W. had thick shoulders and all I could do was press and rub the best I could.

"Good. If thoughts can change Civilization—change Time itself—then they should be able to loosen that rebar in my back. Ah, right there—perfect."

The doctor moved his wheelchair up and I looked right at him from behind C.W.

"You want to talk?" the doctor asked.

"Yea, I do."

"Great, shoot, I have little choice but to listen."

"Doctor, how many daily calories does a human body need to survive?" he asked.

"How many? Boy, you've stumped me on that one."

"Please, I'm deadly serious. We want to avoid any group sickness here. How much food does a person need?"

"To stay alive? I'd say about eight hundred calories and plenty of liquid. But, listen, I've basically been kidnapped, and if the authorities ever found out about this, you'd be in serious trouble. I have no interest in pressing such matters, but I'm a surgeon in Falmouth and I have some very important responsibilities."

"I understand, Dr. Merrithew, but responsibilities are shared by all—"

"Stop it!" the doctor demanded angrily. "Don't patronize me. Who are you anyway? Who? Tell me!"

C.W. raised his hands, telling the guardians to stay put.

"Dr. Merrithew, be sensible. I'm, Lord willing, just doing my thing up here in the mountains with these wonderful people."

"Well, this is quite a thing, this Plentiful—whatever it is."

"Thank you, sir. Coming from a professional man like yourself, I appreciate the compliment. But Dr. Merrithew, again, going back to responsibilities . . . we've got over two hundred people to house and feed here on this sky island, and more on the way I'm told. Can you help us?"

"Help you!" the doctor protested, "What does that mean? Your lieutenant mentioned the same thing earlier. What does—"

"I'm talking about assistance, consultation, perhaps some medical care for the flock."

"Are you out of your mind? Do I look like Albert Schweitzer? Do I?"

"Yes, you do, with moustache and beard. I already like you, and I need your ideas, your knowledge. What kind of doctor are you?"

"If you need a health consultant, hire one."

"What kind?"

"A plastic surgeon."

"Really? Interesting."

"Why would that be interesting? This place has nothing to do with me."

C.W.'s shoulders raised up and threw off my hands.

"How can you think of turning your back on a community like this? You can see the goodness we're trying to achieve here. Anyone with any soul—any heart and intelligence—can see that. Circleville people are a wronged people, and we're trying to move on from a sad situation and do right by the Lord Jesus. You can be a part of that."

"C.W, I have no idea who or what you are, and even if I did, I'm not prone to go following anyone. Believe me, I'm not one of your recruits."

"I think you are, but you just don't see it! Why, I've been re-cruiting, begging, signing up, and cajoling all sorts of people to do all sorts of things for ten years. And you know what I've learned? What I've learned is, after all is said and done, people are simply either good or evil. Good Christian brethren are easy to under-stand, easy to care for. But evildoers, they're a different story. Evil, if left unchanged, can only be treated as evil, watched every minute, controlled, destroyed. That's the way of the universe."

The doctor pointed a finger at C.W. "Don't make threats and act like some fat despot with me."

"Fat and a despot? You have been watching the movies. I'm shocked by your cruel words," C.W. said, chuckling. "Guardians!"

The men all walked forward. "You two take the good doctor back to the clinic house and take care of his foot. Stay at the house permanently. Christina, I feel fine sweetheart, you can go now."

What?, I told myself. Was he changing directions again? Fine, C.W., be that way. I stepped over next to Kenny Wayne.

"Let me at least make a phone call," the doctor pleaded.

"I'm sorry, Dr. Merrithew, we have no phones here."

"Come on, it's illegal what you're doing—I have a wife."

"You work on helping the sickly, Dr. Merrithew. That's your duty. The supplies should already be at the clinic."

Dr. Merrithew was super pissed, and when he turned his wheelchair to leave he glanced back at C.W. "You and I have to talk very soon."

C.W. agreed: "Oh, we'll talk, Dr. Merrithew, believe me, we'll talk a lot. I love to talk. It's my vocation. Now, with no further ado, please get out of here."

RUTH

Those dear boys from Creighton Gardens had been making deliveries to the house for over an hour, using the light from the new lanterns I'd started up. Since my back was nagging me I just let the youngsters do all the moving. But being the sole authority on the little house, I directed them here and there as if I knew where the boxes should be stored, being sure to leave the same little space in the corner of the bedroom for my personal and spiritual needs. I'd been shocked when Trajan said this place was going to be a clinic. There went my special hideaway! But that's the way it is when you're older, all one's cherished places change or disappear.

A bright moon was shining outside and I could just make out the doctor and some others on the Boardwalk. I assumed they were waiting for the gang to finish bringing the supplies from the cable.

"What about this, m'am?"

I squinted at the young man, getting back to business.

"What's the box say, sugar tit? Can you read it?"

He looked at the word like it was an exotic bird. "Pencil—"

These young people today, they're so block-headed, so simple-minded, when it comes to basics.

"Pencil? You mean Penicillin? Put it in the kitchen. All the medication goes in the kitchen."

I didn't know what the doctor was going to say, but that's how I was organizing things. I looked around the rooms, the space getting smaller with every new bag and container being dropped off.

This old house, with its delicate primrose wallpaper, the old-fashioned Handler wall heaters (unusable, unfortunately), and the two-tone inlaid kitchen tile, was a relic from another time, it's walls and foundation probably rotten to the core with termites. Now it was going to be asked to do something beyond its capabilities (just like yours truly!).

The four volunteers finished up their work and no sooner did they say good-bye and set off to the main building than Kenny Wayne, Christina and the doctor appeared in the doorway. Lord Almighty, was there no rest for the wicked?

The doctor hopped along on one foot as he entered, using Kenny Wayne for support. I walked up, putting on my best smile, but couldn't get a word in edge-wise because Kenny Wayne was going on and on about something.

"How could you possibly know about this place? It's in the middle of nowhere," he said. The young man was normally so bashful, I was surprised he was getting all worked up. "When the Apocalypse came, the mine closed down. It just vanished, just like everything else in Circleville."

"Which Apocalypse? There's been so many," the doctor asked mischievously, as if he wanted my attention (and perhaps needed my help?). "You mean when the economy slumped a few years back?"

"No, not then, it was way before that. I mean, yea, the corporations left town, but it was the Government, not the economy. It was like the slow destruction of a way of life and the Government . . . well, the common man just got crushed under its boot heel. And—Ah, just forget it, I can't explain what's in my head. Ask C.W. about it."

Then the door slammed and Christina frolicked by.

"A simple hello might be nice," I said to her, but she disappeared into the kitchen without a word.

Standing awkwardly next to Kenny Wayne, the doctor said, "So, I don't imagine there's any new utilities at our facility here."

"No, unfortunately not, Dr. Merrithew, only lamp light."

"A campsite basically, what fun! I know we've been introduced, but what's your name again?"

"Ruth. I'm Ruth Trundle. How's that nasty leg of yours?"

"Not good," the doctor said, looking around the room, shaking his head. "God, what a nightmare of stuff." He shifted his weight. "Can somebody clear that couch off so I can sit down." We did as he asked, moving a couple of big plastic bags against the wall, then Kenny Wayne helped lower him down onto the battered piece of furniture.

"Bring one of those red boxes over here and let me prop my foot up," the doctor ordered again, without so much as *please.* We did that too, and he lifted his leg onto the box with a grunt.

I could see Christina was already snooping about in the kitchen drawers. That girl was a sneak and I kept my eyes on her every instant. I asked her to bring out two chairs, and when she did, setting them against the living room wall, she remarked, "Midgets must have lived in these rooms. They're sooo tiny."

"No, just regular folks like your grandparents," I said.

Christina walked over to the door of the bedroom. "There's a big hole in the kitchen floor, so watch out, someone might fall into Wonderland."

"Stop it, you silly girl. Now listen, there's a cot in that room if you want to rest."

"I'm cool," she answered to somebody, certainly not me, as she disappeared through the door. What was wrong with that young lady? Always making rude remarks and never looking anyone in the eye. I sat down in one of the chairs. It had been a longer day than I'd expected and my bunions ached something terrible. The doctor settled back on the couch, staring into space, thinking.

He definitely looked like an outsider. Without letting on, I scrutinized him *intuitively,* a habit I'd secretly indulged in for years. I would watch people and imagine them as young children, maybe age five, six or seven, seeing right through their thick adult skin to the seed of what they used to be. At seventy-six, I considered myself something of an expert in this special science. First, I ignored the details of his hair, face, eyes and shoulders, and just caught his total glow, his aura . . . then took that energy back in time, back, back . . . back to whatever appeared and . . . yes . . . OK . . . my, my, what a smartalicky tornado of words and no-good mischief he must have been . . . I bet his Mother wasn't beyond a good spanking with how many times his hand got caught in the cookie jar . . . Coming back to his real face, the man just looked exhausted. You could see the leg pain reflected in his face, but there was an older, deeper pain there as well. Life was slapping his face with its velvet glove, as C.W. used to remark about folks in trouble.

"That goes for you too, Doctor," I said, trying to be a good host. "Make use of that room if you get drowsy."

"I don't like cots," he said. "They smack of the military. I'll just stay where I'm at."

There was a sound at the front door. Paul stepped inside, hauling a bucket, followed by two women carrying a tray of food and some blankets.

"I scrounged some ice for you, Dr. Merrithew," Paul said.

The doctor immediately sat up. "You godsend," he said.

"No, that's you," Paul said, setting the bucket down in front of the doctor.

I didn't bother to get up, but I told Paul to put something under that bucket so it wouldn't get the floor wet, then directed him in placing an old ironing board between two boxes to form a makeshift table for the soup and bread.

"What, no gourmet Wraps?" Dr. Merrithew asked as he rolled his pants leg up, slowly sliding his foot into the slushy water, half-smiling, then gritting his teeth. The women passed the soup around, a single cracker in each bowl, then quickly left to get back to the errands and hungry mouths in the main building. There was a kitchen detail of about fifteen that worked day and night to keep the community fed. No sooner did one meal end than the search for the next meal's scarce ingredients began.

Christina came out of the bedroom and sat down on the couch next to the doctor, acting, oddly enough, like they were old chums. That girl, with her pretty face and cute bottom, was already learning how to get on the good side of the male gender. Kenny Wayne used the chair next to me, and Paul sat cross-legged on the floor by the kitchen door. We sipped our soup and, even though it was too watery, everyone was so hungry that we pretended like we enjoyed it. Making decent soup was so easy that I found it hard to understand why Plentiful's cooks couldn't concoct something with a bit more flavor. If what was in this soup was all the fixings we had, then the Devil must surely be upon us.

I wanted to ask the doctor about his field of medicine, but didn't feel it was proper. Then I scolded myself: Stop being so silly, you're too old to be waiting for anything but Judgment Day. "Doctor?" I ventured.

"Yea," he mumbled over a piece of bread.

"Where do you work 8 to 5?"

"I have a medical practice."

"Like in a hospital?"

"No, I own a clinic in town. It's called About Face."

"Where you work is called that?"

"Yes."

"What kind of medicine is that?"

"Plastic surgery."

"Oh, I see."

Kenny Wayne put his soup bowl down on the floor. "You're one of those guys who changes people's faces?" he asked.

The doctor nodded his head and kept eating, as if he didn't want to say anything more.

"Wow, that's seriously neat," Kenny Wayne exclaimed, and we all looked at each other in unison, as if something strange and amazing had been revealed.

"Maybe you could change the pieces of Paul's puzzle so he doesn't look like Kenny Wayne anymore," Christina suggested slyly.

"Shut up, Christina!" Paul shot back.

"Stop it you two," I warned, before anything got out of hand.

Licking his lips and pushing his moustache back with his finger, Dr. Merrithew said, "Twins—what a wonderful concept, having the same two faces in existence. I'd love it if someone else had my face."

"Ever work on your own face?" Kenny Wayne asked.

"No, my face is fine just the way it is. Can't improve on perfection." He must have been joking, but I couldn't tell for sure.

"Maybe you could erase Ruth's wrinkles?" Christina added.

That was the limit.

"Would you shush and act your age, Christina. Your elders aren't talked to like that."

"OK, OK, don't go all ballistic. I'll be a totally good girl, I promise," Christina said, crossing her heart with her finger. She got up quickly and went into the kitchen again.

"I've never seen no resemblance between Paul and me," Kenny Wayne said matter-of-factly, and I couldn't help but laugh because the two were spitting images of each other. The doctor checked out the twins, and it was like he suddenly decided he was going to communicate with us.

"We all look quite similar really. Take snowflakes for instance. We all know each individual snowflake is completely unique, right? But in reality, in the monotony of their great numbers, they all appear to be very much alike. It's the same with the human face. So, you have to tease out the differences between them, hence surgeons like me."

Christina stuck her head out of the kitchen. "C.W. says, God's greatest invention was the smile."

Dr. Merrithew chuckled to himself, toying with his soup. "I've invented a few in my day," he said under his breath. What did he mean by that? I wondered. That he was God Almighty's equal? Of all the nerve! Well, if he was a non-believer (and he probably wasn't the only one here at Plentiful) he'd come to the right place to learn about the Holy Bible and Scriptures.

I decided to change the subject. "I used to work in a hospital," I announced proudly.

"Did you."

"Well, this was years ago, before my Walter told me to stay home. I was a nursing aide. That's actually where I met C.W., who I believe you just had the pleasure of meeting. He was really just a kid at that time, but even then he was organizing and organizing, trying to secretly get the staff into a union. He was something else, that boy.

But, following his good example, I've learned my Christian duty is to help others, to give alms and do the Good Work, so if I can help you here at the clinic, even with simple things, you let me know."

"Thanks, but no thanks," he answered apathetically. "With some luck, I'll be leaving soon."

"Well, you'll have to talk to C.W. about that," I said.

"Or maybe Trajan," Paul added smartly, like he knew something the rest of us didn't.

The doctor set his soup down on the armrest. "C.W.—Trajan—Trajan—C.W., what is it with all of you? Don't you have anything better to talk about?" Ignoring his meal, he picked up a plastic bag next to the couch and started rifling through it.

"OK, let's check our illustrious inventory? Johnson and Johnson swabs . . . Prozac—Prozac? Now that might come in handy . . . and we've got some Rite Aide tape, Darmant syringes, and what's this?—this is detergent." He dropped the bag and picked up another. "Here we have chewable vitamins, a stethoscope, Whitebright mouthwash, an Internet guide, and . . . red gloves, not medical gloves, but gardening gloves. Incredible!" He tossed that bag on the floor as well, saying, "Too bad we don't have a felt pen, we could make a big garage sale sign—"

But then he stopped, a surprised look on his face. "What do you have there?" he asked. Of all the funny things, Christina was gripping a pair of crutches! She walked over to the doctor. "Here," she said, leaning them up against the couch. He pulled his foot out of the ice water and with Kenny Wayne's help, stood up.

"First, a wheelchair, now this. What's next, a magic carpet?" He grabbed the crutches. "Where'd these come from?"

"In like a broom closet," Christina said. Dripping all over the floor, he placed the crutches under his arms and took a step or two with his injured leg swinging, then walked back and forth a bit. Christina stood there like a tall sunflower, so proud of herself, her cheeks blushing red as an apple.

"That'll work," the doctor said. He leaned them against the wall, then took his position back on the couch, putting his miserable foot back in the ice water.

"I saw some Codeine. Do you want some?" I asked.

"Fantastic, the more I forget, the better."

Since Christina was being such a busybody, I told her where the medication was located in the kitchen. She brought it out to the doctor and he took two 600 milligram tablets. The poor dear, I noticed his hands were shaking as he tore the packets apart. "This better not make me throw up," he said. Kenny Wayne picked through a pile of bedding and found an old ragtag sleeping bag and a couple blankets, then stepped over and spread them across the doctor's lap.

"I have to sleep. I'm half gone," the doctor said, pulling the bag up snug around his shoulders. Evidently he was going to keep his leg in the ice water. "Or maybe I'm already dead, I can't tell," he whispered.

"But wait a second," Paul objected. "I thought we were gonna talk about the clinic? Plan things out."

"Leave me alone, I don't care about the clinic," the doctor said, exhaling deeply.

I stood up. "Paul, skiddaddle now, the doctor's tired." But he kept insisting: "Ruth, if he doesn't give a hoot about the clinic, Trajan's gotta know."

I was about to correct him when the doctor spoke up. "Paul, after that Codeine fix, you tell your boss that Ruth here has been promoted to the position of medical director." I laughed. "I'm afraid I'm a little dimwitted for that," I said, but the doctor didn't respond.

I noticed Peter nodding at Kenny Wayne, telling him it was time to go, so I followed the boys over to the front door. I went up to Kenny Wayne and grabbed his face in my hands, and he let me shake his handsome jaw affectionately, just grinning cute as can be. Then I turned to Paul. "Come on, Grandma, cool it," he complained, turning away.

"You shush now. Paul, listen to me, you get together any shelving you can. Anything made out of wood or metal, anything that boils water or keeps things cold. We have to take care of the sick here at Plentiful, and this is the spot where that stuff is needed. Bring it tomorrow when the doctor's all rested, OK?"

Paul turned away impatiently. I didn't know when or how, but this twin had sure developed a selfish streak. "Whether he's rested or not, it don't seem like the doctor's on the same page as us," he fussed.

"Just pray for his help, Paul. The Kingdom of God is bestowed on those who pray each and every day. Have you been?"

"Yeah, I been talking with the Lord, so don't worry about it," he answered. He wanted to get rid of me and glanced at Kenny Wayne to do it.

"What's wrong with you?" he asked his brother.

"I ain't going across the street," Kenny Wayne said shyly.

Paul pushed his brother's shoulder. "What you talking about?"

"I'm gonna crash here in the living room."

"Whatever—Christina come on, let's go."

Paul stared across the room like he was expecting an immediate response from the girl. Was she staying at Trajan's house too? I didn't approve of that. I looked at her and could tell she wanted to stay put. "You stay here with us, doll, there's plenty of room," I said.

But to my surprise, she didn't pay me any mind. Closing the door of the kitchen, she obediently walked across the room, then, without so much as good-bye, stepped out the front door, Paul following behind.

SHAWNTE

I'd been hustling since sunup, and sunup in a lonely place like this, with people lying around everywhere, was hard to take. After my last run through the tables, when I picked up all the bowls from the morning oatmeal, I sneaked back into the kitchen and rested my sore dogs. These cheap kicks (I didn't have time to grab my bling bling pair before the Exodus) were killing my toes, so I untied the shoelaces and let em breath.

I was getting tired of this kitchen routine, tired of planning menus, cooking, setting and collecting dishes, and dumping trash into the canyon. And, believe you me, I'd started keeping tabs on how this Plentiful thing was bouncing, keeping track of who was doing what, when. Was it just my fellow niggas from the Riverside who were doing all the deep cleaning? Was the script here the same as down below? At last count, there were eighteen brothers and sisters living here, and I was sure gonna keep close track of their moves to find some answers to my questions.

I looked out at all the people under the mile-high ceiling. This old building was a huge damn place, bigger than any spot I'd ever been in, except maybe the County Courthouse on 5th Street. But it was sure looking smaller and smaller with more people calling it home. Everyone was listening to Charles do his Morning Glory routine on the stage. What Glory was he talking about anyway, that's what I'd like to know? That Charles, he was the ultimate grandmaster flash of ceremonials. Nobody, not Ludakris, not Lil Kim, no one, climbed higher ground than he did. C.W. just liked to hear himself talk, and Trajan, well, he got downright nervous in front of folks, but Charles just loved to sell the sun to the moon and change the constellations with all that Bible preaching. But I'd come to the conclusion that showing goodness, only goodness, didn't mean that much in this world. It was more important to know your strength; muscle, and more muscle to back it up, that kept it blazin.

I checked the helpers cleaning the tables. All the men and women were flashing variations on the same dress theme: blue overalls, white T-shirts, and red-checkered bandannas (for just the neck now, not doo-rags to be used with a skully). Where was the iced-out jewelry or blackberry nail polish or freaky weaves? No-where, that's where, just every soul trying to look like the Pope Street posse. I mean, my brother used to wear overalls when he worked on Papa's Buick, but that was the only place. And the worst was people imitating C.W.'s hair: high bangs in front, cut close round the sides, and long down the back. Even brothers, some with dreadlocks, wore that shit, which was a crying shame. But like Trajan always repeated, People pledge their love better and squash beefs better when they're in uniform, and I believed him.

Then, through the back entrance, the medicine man came shuffling in on crutches, escorted by his little entourage. Every head in the place turned. Even Charles up on stage had to pause a moment, which I knew he never liked doing, as the group parked at a table against the north wall. I noticed there was an open spot where they were sitting, so, wanting to see up close what the doctor had bakin in the oven, I moved down just as the music kicked in.

A lady with long red hair stepped up and started singing solo, the musicians watching from behind. I assumed the slow ballad was one of C.W.'s originals. People were always mentioning his writing music and all, but to me the hand didn't fit the glove. And, being honest, his songs were just for white folk, the words just letting you inside the mind, but nowhere else, never any hot rhyming or getting wacked out with it. Pretending I was listening, I glanced at the medicine man—he was staring right at me! His hair was combed back neat, like he'd just washed. "Shawnte?" he said real quick. "Shawnte?" I kinda jumped inside. How'd he remember my name? But I just ignored his line of fire, suspicious that Trajan might be watching.

All the people down front—mostly the Starr Road and Pope Street gangs, who were C.W.'s biggest fans—swayed back and forth with their arms around each other as the woman continued her lullaby. Then the musicians got a little groove going, the guitars strumming faster and faster. Christina, who was sitting right next to me, started clapping her hands and smiling. "This is one of my favorites—it's about a hummingbird," she said. Then she sang along in a clear high voice:

> With wings faster than a spinning atom
> Pearly as a sunshine jewel
> You burst free of the fine gold chains
> That forced you down to earth
> For me, you were ruler of the sky.
> Beauty is in the eye of the beholder
> Flitting wild outside any window
> More than any other bird
> True to God's word
> For me, you were ruler of the sky.
> Sweet, holy spinner of quick tales
> For me, you were ruler of the sky.

The same lyric went around one more time, then everybody kept singing la, la, la—la, la . . . la, la, la—la, la . . . la, la, la—la, la . . . When the song finally ended, the applause was so loud that the singer and the musicians got all red-faced. Laughing and blissed out, they walked off the stage just as brother Charles walked on.

Charles raised his arms up, getting the crowd to freak. How can that man always be smiling like he's just been saved! "Thank you, singers, thank you! That was a wonderful way to start the day, just great." He turned on his heels and walked to the front of the stage, which wasn't much higher than us sitting at the tables. "A group of sweet-tongued people like that need a group name, don't you think? How about the Morning Glory Minstrels, or, say, the New Jerusalem Ensemble. Let me know later if you have any ideas.

Ideas, and more ideas—there's just so many possibilities, aren't there? But first things first: C.W., our Messenger of Light, will be with us today."

There was applause everywhere and yelling from the same loyal believers near the stage. I glanced back at the doctor again; he was talking with some dude who'd just sat down by his side. The guy's head was shaved around the sides, like everyone's, but he still had some mean curls on top. The two men traded deep looks, heads nodding.

"What happened in Falmouth?" someone yelled from the other side of the building. The question floated dangerously around the room, touching people's antennas. Mm, Mm, something was bubblin hot!

But Charles just kept his tempo, "C.W. said yesterday was a great success. But I'll let him tell you about that victory later.

I do have two announcements however. The first is that the prayer groups will be reading from Revelations, the last book in the Bible. It's glorious writing. At that time in history—just like this time in our history—whatever was hidden in God's plan was revealed through signs, miracles, and glorious acts. We can talk about each one in more detail.

My next bit of news is, we have three new citizens in our community! They joined our mission yesterday, when our good soldiers descended into the valley . . ."

66

DOLORES

Why we wait so long outside building? What they talk about and sing about and yell about in there?

I check time, but shit, I forget watch in Circleville.

Why I believe Uncle Ilio? He trick me, that chingadera. He say we just going to nice church to eat good food and be with good people for weekend. I think, that sound OK, we losing lease and need help, but now I somewhere on top of mountains with no one I know.

I don't know why, but two soldiers stand near me and other woman and man. The man ask, What we got to do with the meeting?

"You're waiting to get your hair cut, that's what," the soldier say.

"A haircut?" the man ask all surprised.

"Yea, it happens to everyone who lives here—and that's pretty much all of us."

Haircut? What they mean? Get cut inside with all the people? Forget it!

I look down at my hair all the way to waist, thick, shiny. Everybody since I was little girl love my hair. My Papa say, Oh, Dolores, you blessed like a beautiful horse, and I just let grow and maybe trim two times a year and it get so long long long. But I look around at women going by, the soldiers, all have little long hair on neck, but short on sides. No, no, no, that not me!

The big doors open and you hear the people loud. A man lean out and say, "All right, you can come in now." Our soldier look, "OK, we're going down the aisle and walking up onto the stage. Go single file." One soldier go then the woman and man and last me with other soldier behind.

Inside all the people (I no idea so many people!) stand and clap. On left and on right every eye looking close at us. I am scared now and Circleville is million kilometers away. I look for Uncle Ilio, but no idea where.

Up on stage a black man talks: "With each new community member, we rejuvenate ourselves, don't we? I mean, just think of when each of you first came to the Inner City Path of Peace for a helpful sermon. Didn't that inspire you?" He look down at us. "Well, if those words helped your soul, then put your hands together for these New Believers. They're our new Christian offspring." The people yell back loud.

I tip head down and let my hair hang, looking at tables on the wall and the people sitting down.

But un momento ... Who is that? Is Dr. Collin? A blonde girl, men, black lady, sit at table—and Dr. Collin? Is crazy! Why he not at his house with dogs and wife? He get tricked too? I remember Saturday and my stomach drop down to my pussy and all that water and perfume return from before. I keep looking at him down by stage, but can't get his eyes.

"Watch the steps," the soldier yell and we walk up onto wood floor.

The black man shake hands and smile. "Hello and welcome! Let's all of us turn around and face the congregation." We move and look at people. There so many faces my body shake real bad.

"There is much joy in ritual-taking," the man go on. "You've heard me talk about it before—the different phases of Initiation, Appreciation, and Congregation—and we witness them today, here and now."

I don't know what he mean but he talk and talk about hair and people and Christ. Jesus Christ? This place no real church, just people talking. Where the priest and altar and altar boys? Where they give sacrament and go down and pray? No, this just big room.

"Can I have your names?" the man ask.

Next to me is Anna Marie and Ty and each talk about self.

"And you, young lady?"

Me? No, no, no.

"I'm sorry, I didn't hear what you said."

"I Dolores."

"Well, it's a pleasure to meet all three of you. Thank you for hearing the Call and climbing aboard the dream, the reality, that is Plentiful."

We move over to side and man set up chair in middle of floor. He get scissors ready. Oh, my God, they cut hair now!

Anna Marie sit down and the man get behind and cut curls off.

What I should do? Run? Fight? I have no chance no way. I look down at feet. Where Mama and Father now?

I take hair together and throw over shoulder. I touch it and it feel so soft and good . . . when young every morning Mama sing on porch and brush my hair and tie up with bows and I look so pretty everyone in village look at me and smile . . . And Mr. De Leon at market even give me brown sugar drops from barrel my hair so nice. Maybe I just bad woman. Maybe I just be punished for leaving my country and do bad things with men.

Anna Marie stand up and people clap. She happy now with funny hair. Then Ty sit down smiling too. I know Dr. Collin look at me. He see all my body before but my face more red now. I no want him to see me changed. I be so ugly like man that way.

"Your turn now," a voice say.

I look up. Ty he walk over by the woman. His ears stick out like donkey. They bring me to chair and—Uh!—hair on floor and I step to miss it. All the people stare at me when I sit down.

My uncle go to Hell now. I sure never talk to him again! Maybe if I pray something happen but too late now.

I feel pull on head—my hair fall at feet like limb off a tree. My ear cold and loud with noise. And now other side.

Shit, my heart change forever.

SHAWNTE

When the three rookies left the stage with their new doos, Charles started pacing back and forth, raising his hands up in the air like a heavyweight champ. Everyone knew what that shit meant, so shouts went out and hands clapped faster and faster, the noise echoing off the rafters.

Then from outta nowhere C.W. walked out and the place went crazy. He just stood in one spot, center stage, letting the applause rain down.

I gave him the once over because, being honest, I could never look at the man and take him serious. I knew he was a homegrown genius and his heart was in the right place and he was good at shining for the common man, but the problem was still obvious: He didn't have any female touch.

C.W. bowed to everyone, smiling, still accepting the hysterics. "You know, I'm nothing but a mirror of you all," he called out in that high-pitched voice that belonged in someone else's mouth. He walked around a little, sticking his chest out like a damn comedian. "Look, the applause is bouncing right back at you, right where it belongs." He gave a big laugh then he turned his palms down, requesting quiet and getting it.

"Lord Almighty, hold on to that feeling—that blessed love connection—because if you lose that we're all doomed and you can start throwing dirt on us."

When that word "doomed" was heard it seemed like the idol worship stopped and people got serious real quick. "The newcomers, many thanks go out to you—"

Then he stopped in his own mental tracks. He kept thinking, but couldn't quite put his finger on what to say. Again, I put a lens on him; was he in or outta his game today? Trajan raised that Q all the time: Was C.W. for real or was he just loosey-goosey? I knew when he was playing first string the man could talk for hours and sound like Malcolm or Aristotle or Maya, but at other times he just couldn't lace it and would walk away from the congregation without spitting much of anything. We all waited as he ran his fingers through his long stringy hair, staring at his feet. Then, looking up, he got rolling again: "Fellow Christians, friends from all corners of Circleville, I'm not gonna hide anything from you today. We've got a war on our hands, a war of ideas, a war of truth versus evil, and we won't be able to persevere without everyone's love and commitment."

He stopped, then motioned to the side of the stage. A woman brought a chair out and he sat down, already tired of standing.

"Let's all of us, the whole community, deal with first things first. We won the Revolution decisively. We left Circleville and made it here to these beautiful mountains, where we've started anew, without the barbed wire tyranny of The Chameleon. But we face new battles, that's our difficulty, and that's what saps our strength. Now we have to learn to sail under our own power. We need new policies, philosophies, structures and ideas, something more than what we just left behind." He paused, rubbing his hands together, then requested, "Would everyone please sit down."

We all took a minute and settled back, and as we did, I noticed the curly-haired man slip away from the table, but not before finishing his whispering to the medicine man. Who is that mutha fucka anyway?

"What's the first thing we need?" C.W. asked. "What's paramount? It's safety, isn't it? I mean, in my mind, the most complex truths come in simple packages. If we're an independent community, living by our own rules—Christian rules—rules that satisfy all the people, then we have to feel safe and secure in our own beds. If we don't, we're no better than the weakest beasts in the forest.

Here in Plentiful, the Lord up above and Mother Nature are acting as our gatekeepers, and there's no more powerful combination than that. This is our safe haven, where no one, not the Quinikut County Board, not the Devil himself, not Mayor Bateson or the multi-nationals—"

His breathing couldn't keep up with his words and he stopped. Someone get the Elmers, I thought, he's fallin apart again. But, no, he kept his focus.

"—It's a whole new ball game now because of one fact: Three times a day we have to feed ourselves. I'll say that again, because it's important: Three times a day we have to feed ourselves. So, say good-bye to your mega-markets and fat food factories and gourmet bistros, because now we have to practice the forgotten art of self-reliance, using our savior, Jesus Christ, who made bread from stone, as our example."

He waved to the woman again. She brought him a glass of water and he polished that baby off like he had a mighty thirst.

"I've been reading during the day, thinking at night, and it's gotten clear, perfectly clear, exactly what the Chameleon had in store for us, and the trouble we escaped, down in the valley. Think about the Pentagon implanting biometric I.D. data into the human brain. That's one thing we won't have to endure. Think lethal viruses planted in our midst, just like in Africa and India. And, even worse, think about the government controlling the weather patterns? Yes, it sounds preposterous, but, believe me, it's a known fact. The weather, guided by evil government hands, bringing disaster to parts of the country, to communities, that are rebellious and not toeing the line. Well, if that program works, expect some deep autumn snow here on this island real soon!

Answer me—are all of you pagan clones, ready to follow the Feds?"

Voices screamed out, No, no, no.

C.W. sat up on the edge of his chair, his voice going falsetto.

"America's one big shopping mall, where the blind buy crap imported from far away places where workers are abused worse than the workers in our own sweatshops. And I know you know what the government will always tell you: Hurry now, don't miss it, there's a Big Sale on—the Biggest Ever—so buy, buy, buy, to your hearts content!

Yea, America's a shiny apple, no question about it, but it's a shiny apple with a rotten core, and when people understand that, that's when our paradise will be recognized as the beginning, the symbol, of a new era of Christian living. People looking each other in the eye, with Bible in hand. In plain speak, people loving and respecting one another, respecting local labor, with childcare down the street and medical care for the elderly.

So what about it? Do we walk off a cliff into a sea of forced abortions?"

No, no, no, no . . . the voices declared again.

"What about attacks on our 2nd Amendment rights by The Ten? Is that what you want?"

The Starr Heights and Pope Street gangs jumped up, repeating, "Plen-ti-ful, Plen-ti-ful, Plen-ti-ful" and we all joined the chorus.

C.W. waited, milking the alpha buzz his words had achieved. Then, moving on instinct, he stood up and walked off the stage, out into the congregation. He came down our aisle, and, I admit, I was part of the human wave that was drawn to him.

"You all know me," he said, speaking both personal *and* philosophical, "I'm just a simple so-and-so. But I've been praying—and prayer and some hard thinking has led me to answers.

There's a book I just finished. The title is "Making the Best of Basics", by a Christian brother, James Talmadge Stevens. I'll give it to Charles and he can hand it around tomorrow. But Mr. Stevens talks about how to raise crops and animals, how to raise children without schools and provide medical services without high technology—all the kinds of problems we're gonna solve here in the forest.

Going down into the valley yesterday was a good start. We took our due, and now we have some things to help us survive. We were able to get some parts for a wind generator. We got four new 20-pound Sun Ovens. We got a portable water purifier and, of course, a lot of food and water essentials. And, yes, let it be said, we got some new weapons, but only for protection from outside attackers, because who knows when the slimy tentacles of The Chameleon will reach out to grab us?"

Then a lady who was standing near us stepped out into the aisle. Her get-up was kinda different from the others: a pair of khaki shorts and a blue sweatshirt with the word *Saved* on it.

"Excuse me," she asked, "but I have a question. What happened to Freddie Stark?"

The curly-haired guy who'd just been talking to the doctor stood up behind the woman, putting his hand on her shoulder for support.

"What's your name?" C.W. asked.

"Lorraine Faye," she answered. She turned and, over her shoulder, smiled at the man.

"Where are you from, my friend?"

"The Peaks."

"Really, by Sisk Records or the Towers."

"Sisk's, but what—"

"Listen to me," C.W. said, raising his voice and turning so everyone could hear. "I have terrible news. Two men died in Falmouth, one was the man you mentioned, the other was Phil Winningham."

Cries went out from the congregation, then stone-cold silence. People were like they got punched in the stomach and couldn't breathe. My, my, that was the first drawing of blood since Ray Borbon was killed in the riots after the Day-Glo fires. Well, at least C.W. was coming clean.

"But what happened?" the woman kept up, all bent outta shape.

"We went to the heart of the New World Order—the Heritage Bank—and they died in an ambush."

"But who ordered that attack?" the curly-haired man asked loud and clear, stepping in front of the woman. "When did the community ever discuss or approve doing that? Plentiful is supposed to be a place where everyone has a voice, right? I was never asked about any of this. None of us were."

"This woman has already told us her name, what's yours?"

"What difference does it make?" the man said, looking around at the crowd for understanding. "C.W., listen, I can't thank you enough for what you've done. I'm in awe of what's happened this past year, but things aren't—"

"Things aren't what?" C.W. interrupted. C.W always acted like he was just fun and ideas, but, truth be known, he didn't like his rap interrupted.

"With God as my witness, I'm concerned that you can't even reveal your name to the congregation. We all know one another here. It's our tradition to introduce ourselves to each other."

"My name's Bosco Perloff, alright?"

"Thank you, Bosco. We did lose two brave men. We didn't expect violence, we didn't want violence, but we were attacked. It's the tragic, irreversible price we paid for having to supply ourselves with necessities—"

"But, Wise One, everybody knew those guys. They were leaders of this community too; not in your position, but still—Freddie was the best mechanic we had. They were smart and had skills and worked right along with you—and Trajan too—helping build what we have here. But going into Falmouth? Why, anybody would know that's just asking for trouble.

Whatever happened to the Laity Councils that we were going to have? Laity Councils with rotating members, wasn't that the original idea?"

C.W. scowled, then scratched the back of his neck again. He'd had enough.

"It's important that you speak your mind, I appreciate that. But what does the rest of the community think?" C.W. asked, turning in a circle, raising his hands up. "Am I a tyrant in lamb's clothing? If so, I'll have to be accountable, that's all there is to it." C.W. put his hand up to his ear. "Well?"

That Lorraine woman snapped. "You know, you're obstructing what everyone's saying, and that's not fair," she complained, pointing at C.W. "This isn't your own little kingdom, and if it is, then this place is no better than Circleville."

C.W. ignored her, putting his hand to his ear again, "Well, I'm waiting for some other opinions."

Voices started ringing out, especially down front by the stage:

"They're spies, C.W., media spies, don't trust them."

"We love you and need you. We'll always love you."

"Don't pollute the Word—banish the Devils."

"Resource Hour. Let them talk at Resource Hour."

C.W. looked at the man and woman, acknowledging the callers.

"There seems to be a difference of opinion here. But that's OK, that's what Plentiful is all about. Charles, my good man, where are you?"

"Right here, C.W." Charles answered, standing up from his seat on the stage.

"Charles, please meet with Lorraine and Bosco and set up the Laity Councils. Bosco's right, that was something we had talked about."

So, even though the two protesters were still hot and bothered, both agreed to talk with Charles later and sat their butts down.

C.W. strolled down the aisle, feeling his oats again.

"But what our good friends have just said is true, we can't sweep this under the rug. We have to talk about the dead—honor their sacrifices. To accomplish this, there will be a funeral service this afternoon. At four o'clock everyone should gather at the eastern cliffs, then we can pay our due respects to these loyal men who fell in battle."

C.W. kept moving down the aisle as he rapped, and when he got to our table, he stopped.

"After talking about this tragedy, I have something to raise the spirits a little bit, something Plentiful is going to be very, very proud of."

He moved his big ass right next to us, so close that Christina reached out and touched his hand. C.W. winked at her, then turned back to the whole room.

"Good people, Plentiful now has a doctor for medical services."

C.W. motioned for the medicine man to stand up, but Feelgood just stayed put.

C.W. spread out his arms like the Good Shepherd.

"I'm honored to introduce Dr. Collin Merrithew. Dr. Merrithew is a surgeon from Falmouth and he has been good enough to volunteer his time to establish a clinic here. Let's give him a warm Christian welcome."

Nobody quite knew what to do. Some folks clapped, but mostly everyone just chilled, wondering: A doctor? What sky did this guy drop out of?

"Maybe, because of his kind efforts, we can name the clinic after him," C.W. suggested. "The Merrithew Health Clinic. That has a nice ring to it. Do you like the sound of that, Doctor?" But Feelgood looked straight ahead, cold as the ages.

"No comment," he said.

C.W. kept at him. "Well, I've been talking about security and self-sufficiency, and you, you're the foundation of that strength. No more waiting in the corridors at the County Hospital, no more getting turned away." He put his hand on the doctor's shoulder. "You're the angel who will cure our ailments."

The doctor glanced up at C.W., his eyes fuming—then, bam, suddenly he stood up and grabbed his crutches and started bangin into shit to get away. He stumbled up the aisle towards the back exit. Good God, I thought, the guy's snappin big time. I was sure the guardians were gonna stop him at the back doors, but he just waved them off and split out the building.

Everybody looked around, shaking heads, whispering. And wouldn't you know, just like clockwork, that Christina girl slipped away from the table and trailed the medicine man outside.

Where was Trajan? I needed to powwow quick. I checked out the stage. He and C.W. and Charles were already discussing the buzz and how to lace it back together. They broke up and Charles walked out and faced the crowd. "Let's bring this meeting to a close," he announced in a booming voice. "Certainly, we need to find out what's troubling the doctor, but, first, let's pray. I think we all know the fourth devotion from Psalms, so let's begin . . ."

CHRISTINA

I couldn't see Dr. Merrithew anywhere. Why'd he bail like that? Seeing him struggle up the aisle with those crutches made me just brush off what C.W. was saying and try to help.

"Hey, Doctor," I yelled, "where you at?" I ran farther out across the field. There he is! He was standing over by an old pump and some metal tanks. I hurried towards him and as I walked up, he asked out of the blue, "Where's that tram from here?"

"Over there," I said, pointing to the far side of the building, amazed he was so turned around. "Dr. Merrithew?"

"What is it?" he asked in a Neanderthal voice.

"C.W. is just trying to help is all. It's no big—"

He wacked the tank with his crutch. "Stop. Don't say another word." The tank echoed and I stepped back, scared. "Christina, look at me now. Do you know of any trails around here, trails where you can hike down into the canyon?"

"No, not that I know of, only the path to the headquarters."

"I was afraid of that," he said. Then he looked over my shoulder. "Here they come."

I glanced back and saw Trajan and the others running straight at us. Behind them, big black shadows moved along the side of the building, like pieces of nighttime that had escaped the sunlight. Clouds did somersaults in the sky.

"God, I hate this man," Dr. Merrithew said.

"Well, Jesus says not to hate anybody," I said, sounding like a Sunday School teacher. "But I bet I know what you mean."

Trajan rushed up, followed by Paul, the big black woman, and two guardians. "Where you going so fast?" Trajan asked.

"Just enjoying the mountain views," the doctor said, and you could tell by how his shoulder twitched that he expected to get hit again. "I'm sure you can relate to that, being from the flatlands."

"Keep your mouth shut," Trajan demanded. In a sitch like this I just looked down at my feet and listened to the voices. "You don't go anywhere from now on unless I say you can. Got it? The clinic and the main building, that's it."

"Good host, whatever—"

"Man, did you hear me? Shut your yapper!"

I got a push on the shoulder. It was Paul, nodding at me, reminding me to listen. My lips spoke silently: Shut up.

"Christina, back inside," Trajan insisted, pointing for me to go.

I didn't really want to leave the doctor, but orders were orders. I caught Dr. Merrithew's eye, then walked away. Behind me, I could hear the doctor and Trajan arguing louder and louder. It made my heart pound with fear, so I ran as fast as I could back to the entrance of the building. I stepped behind one of the big metal doors, listening, inside, to Charles' deep voice and the crowd humming like a beehive. I checked the field again. Dr. Merrithew was waving his crutches, helpless as a grasshopper smothered in ants, then they just dragged him away.

What are they gonna do with him? To find out, I crept around the side of the building, following them down the Boardwalk. I thought they'd, like, be going to the clinic, but, no, they dragged him like a sack-of-potatoes across the street and shoved him through the front door of Trajan's house. Without thinking twice, I ran over and crouched down under a window by a stack of bricks and tools. I could hear all sorts of thumping sounds coming outta the wall.

Thinking of being in that house paralyzed me. I started biting my nails something fierce, my mind going to the races again. No, no, no, I said to myself, but was helpless to stop it . . . *I wanted to be invisible, to disappear into thin air, to be anywhere but here, but . . . The cars arrived late at night . . . up above where they couldn't be seen . . . somehow they knew I was sleeping here alone in the house by the lake . . . a decision had been made . . . dressed in white the visitors silently descended the narrow steps . . . then at every door and every window a face staring at me . . . eyes glowing . . . "We're ready. Are you prepared to—"*

Then a voice snapped me out of it. "Use the tape. Use the tape," someone repeated. I sucked up my fear and raised my head. There was a curtain over the window, but down in the corner I could get a clear view.

They had the doctor in a chair. He was fighting like a wild child, grabbing at anything and anyone he could get his hands on. Paul had a roll of tape and was trying to get his arms behind the back of the chair, but the doctor held onto a fistful of Shawnte's shirt. Then Trajan went to work like a cowboy wrestling a steer. He just slammed the doctor to the floor and had the guards hold him while he taped his arms and ankles. Then the woman handed Trajan a pair of scissors.

I can't believe it, I thought, my stomach jumping, the doctor's gonna get clipped in private! Right then I realized that Dr. Merrithew would never be a part of Plentiful, never really join with us and learn to love our mission, and, God forgive me, but I wanted to sink the scissors right in Trajan's back because of it.

Who could I talk to about all this? Who wanted to know? No one really—they were all in the building and probably didn't care anyway. I didn't want to be alone, but I didn't want to see any more of this either, so I escaped into the trees.

RUTH

After I strolled back from the long Morning Glory meeting I found Dr. Merrithew already at the clinic and was shocked by what I saw. I don't know when or how it happened, but his beard and hair had been shaved off. Blood from little cuts had dried on his face and he was in a mood fit for the Devil.

And just like it always was with my Walter, when a man had a familiar beard or moustache, then lost it, his face always had some odd characteristic that you never dreamed of, and so it was with the doctor. His cheeks were rough, maybe from acne as a teenager; his head seemed smaller too, his complexion pale.

He sat on the couch and didn't pay any mind to his injured leg like he had the days before. I hovered around, asking him this and that, but no, not a peep from the man. The poor soul, I didn't know what to do for him and was afraid he wouldn't be willing to manage the clinic as planned. So, as he stared into nothingness, I made busybodies out of Pribble, Kenny Wayne, and Christina, and we made some real progress in getting things organized. The medication was arranged alphabetically in the kitchen cupboards, with the top flap of each box neatly torn open for proper access, and the name circled with a magic marker. Any and all medical equipment went into the bedroom. Since we had no idea how to use most of it, we waited for the doctor's consultation in the use of syringes, stethoscopes, blood sugar kits, asthma pumps, saline lines, and all the rest. We cleared the foyer of old furniture, and a newfound card table and chairs was set up at Dr. Merrithew's end of the room.

To find a place for a container of Vitamin B I'd discovered, I stepped into the kitchen. Christina was already there—sneaking water!

"What are you doing, young lady? That's not your private drinking fountain. It's for clinic use only."

Christina turned away and, tipping her head, emptied the cup she was holding.

"Did you hear me, put it back right now!"

"OK, OK," she said. "Don't have a cow." She threw the cup in the sink.

I walked up behind her. "That will be moved, so don't try it again." She nodded, then looked away with big, sad blue eyes, stroking her long blonde hair, always stroking her hair. Suddenly,

I felt terrible about my harsh words because now I could see that she was the one who needed help, who needed water.

"Would you like me to brush your hair, sweetheart?" I asked, trying to touch her shiny mane. She pulled back and swatted at my hand.

"What's wrong, little lamb?" I asked. "Let me make a nice braid."

Christina kept her eyes down. For a moment I thought she might start crying, but her troubles seemed somehow beyond tears.

"I wish I could make you a stack of waffles with crushed walnuts and a dollop of whipped cream and some loganberry syrup on top. And you could finish it all off with a tall glass of fresh-squeezed orange juice. But, honey, you know I don't have the groceries."

Christina glanced at me with a little smile. I grabbed her hand and held on tight.

"What's wrong now?"

"Everything."

"Please, don't say that. I love you and Jesus loves you, and His love is everlasting."

"I'm not even singing for C.W. anymore . . ."

"You and your singing and fancy words—but that's not it, that's missing the point. It's staying across the street, not C.W., that's bothering you. It's clear as day. Tell me, where do you sleep when you're over there?"

Christina pulled her hand away. "Stop crushin on it. You couldn't do anything about it anyway."

Her words hurt my pride something terrible and I needed all my strength to keep *my* emotions in check. But Christina stepped up to me, "I'm sorry I said that, Ruth. That was mean."

"You're probably right dear, but, still, you should be staying here at the clinic."

"I can't. I don't even know if the doctor likes me. Does he?"

"Of course he does. You're such a hard worker, with such a big heart."

She stroked her hair again, fragile as a flower.

"I'll pray for you, dear, and we'll see what the Lord can do."

Then our heads were turned by a loud voice coming from the living room.

"Break time, break time! The boss says, Take five," the voice proclaimed.

"It's Pribble acting goofy," Christina whispered.

"Well, you go ahead. Do you need any more water, honey? If not, I'm going to put it back under the sink."

"No, I'm fine," Christina said, then slipped away.

In the living room we all sat and watched Bosco, who always seemed to be doing something with his hands, put together a shelf in the foyer with some cement blocks and pieces of wood. After he finished the project, he came over and joined us.

"Whoa, what happened to you?" he asked Dr. Merrithew. "Got attacked by a flying razor, huh? I bet I know—"

"Change the subject," the doctor interrupted.

Bosco put up his hands defensively. "No problem, I'd be angry too," he said.

"Anger doesn't come close to describing what I feel," the doctor added without emotion. During an awkward silence, the doctor kept his eye on Pribble, finally asking, "Pribble, do you ever write letters or anything to your family or friends in Circleville?"

"Naw, not really. I ain't got any kin."

"But how do you communicate with the outside world?"

"We cross over the cable."

"But what about a computer or the Internet or a phone? I mean, don't some of you have to talk to people down below?"

"C.W. might have a cell phone—maybe. I think he kinda keeps it a secret. But there sure ain't no phone booths up here."

The doctor, with his new face, looked around at all of us. "You know, I can't expect anyone here to be aware of it, but I'm a doctor with people who are dependent on my care. My being up here can cause a grandmother or a child to become ill or even die. Their lives are literally in my hands, do you understand that? I'm a doctor, and every minute that passes puts my patients in greater and greater danger."

"What's gonna happen to those sick people?" Kenny Wayne asked.

"I don't really know. I'd like to at least *talk* with my patients, maybe refer them to an associate."

The doctor was in a nasty dilemma, no doubt about it, but none of us had any bright recommendations about how to solve it, so we all just kept quiet and listened to the blue jays fighting in the trees outside.

But Dr. Merrithew continued: "Pribble, besides Ruth, are you the oldest person here at Plentiful?"

"Yea, I suppose. I ain't done any math, but I guess you could say I'm the senior man."

"How old are you, if you don't mind my asking?"

"Fifty-two, and proud of it," Pribble answered. He breathed into his hand and polished his heart, grinning.

"In your prime, huh?"

"That's right, you got it. I like the sound of that!"

"How did you get your position here?"

"I knew C.W. and Trajan since they was kids. Matter of fact, I'm practically older than both them put together."

"Really? And those greenhorns are telling you what to do?"

"I guess—what you gettin at?"

"Well, it just seems that Trajan and C.W. are calling the shots, that's all. That must be hard for you."

"Pribble's a lieutenant," Kenny Wayne said.

"A lieutenant?" the doctor said with amazement. "That status doesn't mean much with a general and a king above you. No one wants to be low man on the totem pole."

"But that ain't true—I have my say," Pribble let it be known.

"In those Laity meetings that C.W. was promising this morning, is that what you mean?"

"No, that ain't what I mean. What I mean is, I can tell people what to do. I can give orders and have em followed. I'm not one of them nobody recruits that was pulled off the street."

Kenny Wayne started giggling, then Christina laughed too. I had to keep from smiling myself, Pribble was acting so simple-minded and foolish.

"What you laughing at?" Pribble asked, his voice getting worked up. "I know stuff you'll never know."

"Like what, Mr. Smarty Pants? Tell us," Christina demanded.

"I can't say right now, but I know the truth and you don't."

"Right, King Pribble," Kenny Wayne said, then he and Christina started taunting in unison, "King Pribble, King Pribble—"

"Shut up! What C.W. said this morning, was that the truth, huh? Was it? Well, I know if it was and you don't?"

Kenny Wayne continued with his teasing, "Roll out the red carpet for—"

"Be quiet," the doctor ordered, and Kenny Wayne stopped his antics.

Pribble had his head down, rubbing his ear. "Even Christina don't even know," he said, trying to smile, as if smiling would make right the situation. Christina got more and more serious as Pribble spoke his mind. "I'm the only one. That talk about the men getting killed, that wasn't nothin but a speech. That's shit words, pretend words. I know who killed em."

"I believe you, Pribble—I think you probably do know more than the rest of us," the doctor said. "But there's a difference between knowing what's wrong and having the guts to say so and doing something about it. To get respect, to really earn it, you have to be strong enough to act on your own."

Pribble's eyes got big and scared, then ants hit his pants and he rushed into the kitchen to be alone. I could see him clearly from where I was sitting. He gripped the window ledge angrily and seemed to be talking to himself. The doctor slowly got up, adjusted his crutches, then went into the kitchen too, closing the door behind him.

"What are you teasing Pribble for?" Christina asked Kenny Wayne.

"You were doing it too," he fired back.

"So? I'm always giving him a hard time."

Then, without so much as a word, Pribble bolted out of the kitchen and practically knocked Bosco over as he ran out the front door. From out the front window I could see him run off down the Boardwalk.

Dr. Merrithew came back to the couch.

"What's eating him?" Bosco asked, cracking his knuckles.

84

"He's having a psychological breakdown," Dr. Merrithew said matter-of-factly, sounding like we were in a real meeting. "What all of you are doing here in the mountains is abnormal and illegal—"

"Naw, Pribble's always been like that," Kenny Wayne said. "I think he was in a hospital himself, wasn't he?"

"I wouldn't be surprised," Dr. Merrithew said. "But what's he keep talking about? All this hysteria about people getting killed—"

"I don't know," I said, not wanting to even think about what Pribble meant.

"Christina, who's he blaming?" Dr. Merrithew asked.

"You're asking me? You gotta be kidding," Christina said.

"Christina," the doctor persisted, "you were there, weren't you?"

"In Falmouth? Yea."

"Did you see what Pribble saw?"

"I don't know, I don't know, I don't knoooow."

"Alright, calm down. Let's just drop the whole thing," Dr. Merrithew said, sitting back in a huff, retreating into his own thoughts.

With my energy running low, I tidied up a few things and went into the bedroom, said a short prayer, then layed down. But I couldn't get out of my mind how the doctor had used the word "abnormal"; why, he'd even claimed Plentiful wasn't law-abiding.

I breathed deep and adjusted the blanket I was using as a pillow, my muscles aching something fierce. What was normal anyway? C.W. had a saying, Normal was the shoes on people's feet, and everyone's size is different. I believed him, and wanted him to be right, but was he? I just didn't know anymore. Yet looking back over my own life, I knew one thing for certain: Without the Word of God, everything was eventually corrupted by the immorality of the world.

I woke up to loud voices and noise in the front of the house. When I went to see what the commotion was all about, there was a big box in the doorway—a box like a piece of furniture would be delivered in—and Trajan, Peter and two guardians were struggling to push it inside.

Kenny Wayne and Bosco immediately jumped into the mix and started pulling the cumbersome thing. Trajan was in a fury, ordering everyone here and there, and when they finally got it moved in, he walked over to the doctor. "Merrithew, we gotta talk."

At first, the doctor ignored Trajan, torturing him with a little silence, then he finally spoke up, "Trajan, we are talking. Make yourself clear."

"I mean in private, just you and me."

"Listen, you're in my clinic now, where communication is golden. This is my staff. There are no secrets here. If you want to talk, talk."

"OK," Trajan said, giving us the once over before continuing, "In this box here, there's two bodies. They're here for the funeral. That clear enough?"

The doctor stared at the wall.

"The men whose funeral it is, this is them," Trajan repeated.

The doctor immediately took pains to get up, using Bosco's assistance. "When did they die?" the doctor asked.

"You know when: yesterday, just like C.W. said. But can you dress a dead man, cause that's what they want?"

"Dress? No, I'm a surgeon, Trajan, not a mortician. There's a difference."

"Well, they gotta be dressed up."

"What are you talking about?" Dr. Merrithew tried to touch what used to be his beard.

"I don't know really, it's C.W.'s plan," Trajan answered, running his hands through his thick hair. "He and Charles are gonna talk at the cliffs. We're gonna sing, then drop the men into the canyon."

Dr. Merrithew slowly shuffled over to the box, pulling all of us along out of morbid curiosity. Trajan kept talking to the doctor's back, "Like on a boat, Merrithew, official-like. It has to look good—"

The doctor ignored Trajan again and asked for the flashlight we'd found in the kitchen that morning, and Christina quickly retrieved it. "Someone open the top," he ordered, turning the flashlight on. "I can't bend forward far enough."

All the men glanced at each other, hesitating, and when Bosco stepped forward, Christina moved right in front of him, saying, "Here, I can do it."

"No, Christina, absolutely not," the doctor insisted, blocking her way. "Bosco, go ahead." So Bosco pulled apart the flaps and opened the top.

"You're going to need a table or something," Trajan reasoned.

"Hold your horses," Dr. Merrithew warned, "I want to see something first."

The doctor moved up to the side of the box, raising the flashlight. Everybody tried to pretend there was no smell, but there was. All we could do was read the doctor's eyes as he checked inside. Shining the light here and there, his gaze held steady, but his lips tightened up. Then he quickly turned away.

"Too much time has passed," he concluded grimly. "Close it up."

"What's that? We gotta bury em, there's no choice," Trajan argued.

"Rigor mortis has set in. They're like pretzels because they've been stored in a box, for what reason I won't get into."

No one could say a thing, from shock. Christina started sobbing, so Kenny Wayne walked over and put his hand on her shoulder, then he broke down too.

"Merrithew, it's up to you—do something!" Trajan commanded. "The whole place is waiting."

You could tell the doctor had no intention of doing anything in agreement with Trajan. Why, you could package the hate between those two men.

"We don't have any coffins, Trajan," I added, trying to ease the tension, "so I don't know how we could have a traditional ceremony anyway."

"Just bury them like that," Bosco suggested.

"Yea? How?" Trajan asked.

"Bury them in the box, together. That still looks formal."

"Yes, you could use that red curtain we found in back," I said, remembering the paper bag it had been stored in. I looked at Christina, in hopes that she could get it for me, but she was still too upset.

"Do whatever you want, I have no solutions," the doctor said, moving back to the couch.

So, it was a good thing I'd taken a nap, because I had to muster my energy and get down to the business of wrapping the box in white sheets then draping it with the old fuzzy velvet material (which, thank God, had been put in moth balls).

Nobody said it, but I could tell everyone was relieved that we didn't have to view and, goodness gracious, handle the dead martyrs.

Two more guardians showed up, and Bosco, Peter and Kenny Wayne joined the four men in getting the box outside. Using some 2x4's found in the yard, they lifted the box up onto their shoulders like the Pharoah's own slaves, then moved slowly down the Boardwalk towards the trail.

I considered just staying at the clinic and resting. My thoughts were heavy from all the strife—and now this funeral—here at Plentiful. I couldn't understand how things had come to this. But out of respect for the dead, I went and joined the others.

But we were late arriving at the cliffs. The whole community was already there waiting, sitting along the canyon edge and all through the rocks up the hillside.

SHAWNTE

We'd just started singing "The Sun Will Shine Brighter" when all the musicians just kinda came to a halt. The whole congregation turned their heads and followed a buzz up the trail.

A group of men were carrying a big square red thing on their shoulders. I had no idea what it was. They moved carefully down through the crowd, which separated in two to let the men pass. Following behind, Trajan came with the doctor in his wheelchair and the clinic ladies.

"Is that supposed to be a coffin?" a man close-by asked. For real? I asked myself. It was covered in sheets and looked like a

Christmas present gone bad, but, yea, I think the man was on the money.

The men carrying the box ran outta gas and had to stop. Charles, who'd been standing by C.W. at the cliffs, immediately hustled up to them. He went around the box, shaking each dude's hand, then looked out at all of us. "To honor the deceased," he said in a solemn voice, "let's start our song again." So, because it was a sad affair, we all totally lost gravity and took it right to the top with our best voices:

> *How warm the sun when the clouds return to water*
> *How bright the moon when nighttime sets it free*
> *How light our sins on the shoulders of dear Lord Jesus*
> *From high atop the tallest tree*
> *Oh! Praise dear Lord Jesus.*

As if moved by the holy singing, the men raised the big box on their shoulders again and stumbled forward. And Charles moved right long with them, leading the second verse:

> *If brothers die by fire and sisters crumble and weep*
> *Then we must cross the Parquat River*
> *Where the water's cold and deep*
> *On the shoulders of dear Lord Jesus*
> *Who walks upon the water*
> *We'll smite the Devil in his sleep*
> *Oh! Praise dear Lord Jesus.*

Just as the men slowly, dangerously, set their burden down by the canyon edge, I walked up behind some rocks and came down near where Trajan was standing with his posse. I slipped a few corn flakes in my mouth, then checked Feelgood's new face and doo. Lord have mercy, I thought, he shoulda just cooperated with us from the get go.

C.W., who'd been gazing out into the wild blue yonder, finally walked over and stood in front of the coffin. Everybody hushed . . . the big sky, the empty canyon, the tall trees rising up, made us all look like a herd of scared little animals.

89

"These are our friends—Circleville friends—and fellow citizens here at Plentiful. We honor them in this ceremony because we honor ourselves. We honor them because we come from the same streets, the same old houses, sat in front of the same tired teachers, and breathed the same dirty air from Aurora/Slat."

Nobody wanted to give up a laugh and ruin the serious occasion, but there was still a murmur of acknowledgement when that stinking refinery was mentioned.

"Even those who do God's work, who are just and moral and work for the good of the community, get cut down by Satan's hand, that's just history repeating itself, injustice after injustice. If I knew my Bible better, I'd quote something right now, but I don't have Charles' gift with the Scriptures."

C.W. looked at Charles, who tipped his head a little, then continued, "I knew Phil Winningham and I knew Freddie Stark. I used to see Phil using the computer at Malarkey's at all hours of the night, and both of them donated time at the food bank feed last year. Nice hardworking guys those two; never hurt a fly."

C.W. moved over to the big coffin, which came even with his chest. Then he reached out and put his hand on the red covering, and, I don't know what it was, but he just sanctified the moment right then, sanctified it and made it righteous by touching the dead, touching them with love and respect, right in broad daylight. I had to give it to the man, that was a beautiful thing.

Keeping his hand there, he went on: "We can rise up in anger about their deaths. Anyone would be justified in doing that. But that would only be bringing the barbarians into our hearts. Asking why, why, why, can go on forever and we should avoid that. Using these men's example, we have to build something greater, and by God's grace and our own muscle, we're gonna do it.

Since we live on an island now, separate and independent, this open canyon is like our sea, and these two men will be pushed into the sea as their everlasting resting place. Plentiful—a great ship under sail—will be protected by the sea around us, and that same sea will protect our two heroes. This is the most Christian way to honor them.

Can the men who carried the coffin help put these men to rest? And Charles—a prayer please."

The carriers crowded round the back end of the box as Charles began leading the Lord's Prayer. Inch by inch, the men moved the coffin towards the edge and as "kingdom come, thy will be done" left our lips, the box tipped and went bottom up, totally disappearing. It was like we all blinked at once, half-speaking the prayer, half-waiting, waiting for some sound . . . but nothin came, zip, just the ghost-rattle of the wind in the trees.

Staring at the empty space where the box used to be, people started moanin and spazin out. While the grieving spread, I noticed Charles and the musicians walk away single-file through the crowd, heading towards a small building beyond the rocks that I'd never seen before.

C.W. went on, "Please, everyone, just stay where you are for a moment. I want you to close your eyes and take a private moment to say good-bye to our heroes."

He stepped over and stood where the coffin had been. "Give thanks—their spirits are flying away."

In a minute the musicians returned, with Charles bringing up the rear. But now you could hear a voice screaming: waaaaa, waaaaa, waaaaaaa. As they all moved down to the canyon edge, C.W. started talking again, "Brothers and sisters, I apologize. I've been keeping a secret from you. But it had to be kept until just the right moment."

C.W. walked over to Charles. "Death only leads to life, perhaps a greater life and a chance at redemption," he said, then we watched as he took a *baby* from Charles' arms.

C.W. held the little tike over his head, grinning from ear to ear, then started walking through the crowd. "It's Plentiful's first newborn—and, for better or worse, it's a boy," he exclaimed.

A baby! my thoughts screamed. This shit's bananas. Whose gonna feed a baby up in these climes. That poor thing's tummy is already crying out.

"Whose is it?" a voice yelled from the other side of the field.

C.W. stopped in his tracks. "I'm glad you asked. You all know how many of our brethren died in the Day-Glo fire, I know you do. I could name all 67, but there's no need because this funeral honors Freddie and Phil. But there was one woman, Florence

Clayborn, who died in the fire not long after giving birth. The baby, whose name is Benedict, or Bennie as I like to call him, happened to be at the hospital when the fire occurred, so he survived. We brought him back so he could be raised with folks his mother knew."

Charles came up behind C.W, then called out, "Behold, the Lord has brought unto us a child, our own little baby Moses. Let's all pass by and greet this special boy and wish him well before walking back. And praise God on high."

So, even though the baby was still screaming to high heaven, one by one the congregation stepped up to recognize and honor the infant. Waiting my turn, I caught Trajan's eye. He winked at me, instantly scheduling a meeting for later that night.

CHRISTINA

After the funeral, at the headquarters, I told C.W. I was totally an infant when it came to babies, but he kept saying I'd make a perfect nanny because of my nice personality. Because Bennie was coughing all the time, he needed special care at the clinic, and I was the only one he trusted to be with him. Charles suggested that the baby stay with other women in the community, but C.W. wouldn't go for it. No, it had to be someone in the inner circle and, sure enough, that meant me. Getting a headache from all the stupid words, I finally stopped protesting, saying, "Do what you want, I surrender. But you gotta give me some help, OK?"

Dr. Merrithew and Bosco were on the couch talking when I arrived at the clinic with Bennie. I felt kinda awkward and didn't want to interrupt, but Dr. Merrithew greeted me, "Christina, come in and sit down. What do you have there?"

"I got the baby with me."

"Giving him the grand tour?"

"No, C.W. wants him to stay here."

Bosco slapped his knee and laughed.

"Here? Why here?" the doctor asked.

"I don't know. He says Bennie has a cold—he's coughing a lot—and might get sicker if he doesn't get help."

Bosco was immediately all hot and bothered by the plan and complained about what it meant to have the baby around, and the doctor agreed. I didn't really want to mention it, but *anybody* was better than having C.W. take care of Bennie. It wasn't just that he was a guy, he just didn't have it together. Like, when I was at the headquarters, C.W. told Charles to take the baby outta the room cause he needed inspiration time and the baby's crying was driving him crazy. He sounded all weird, repeating, Plentiful's reached a point of no return, everyone out, everyone out.

"You better move on Bosco," Dr. Merrithew said, like he was warning him about something.

"Yea, you're right," Bosco agreed, standing up. "But are you accepting this babysitting arrangement?"

"Bosco, I accept everything now. Do you have any other bright suggestions or democratic alternatives? The clean-shaven pediatrician, the mortician, that's me. But listen, if this baby has to be around, somebody has to bring food, milk, blankets, and something for diapers. Talk to Ruth, she's got all the connections." Bosco said that he'd take care of it and left.

I just stood there in the middle of the room with the doctor watching me. Bennie gurgled and breathed deep and I looked down at his darling face, deep in sleep. It was amazing because I could actually feel his breathing, his Life, right there in my arms! But what was I supposed to do with him now?

"Christina, I'm warning you, we're not going to sleep much tonight."

"Yea, babies have to eat all day and night, huh? Dr. Merrithew, can you hold Bennie. I'll—"

"No, no, you stick with it. My mood is not congruent with this."

"But he's sick—"

"C.W. is sick to bring a baby here, that's who's sick."

"But he doesn't want the baby in a foster home."

"It's dangerous, what if the baby dies up here."

This man was sooo on my nerves. Why was he always throwing a wet blankie on my stuff? "Well, you have to know more about babies than I do."

"No, I don't. I don't have children, Christina, I know nothing, hear me, nothing, about babies." Dr. Merrithew was getting so steamed I was afraid to hand Bennie to him. Maybe he was no better at this than C.W. But my arms were aching and the doctor must have picked up that I was at the end of my rope, because he finally said, "Here, give him to me. See if there's something in the bedroom we can use for a crib."

He took Bennie under his tiny arms and set him on the box he'd been using to support his leg. His little head tipped up and down then he opened his dreamy eyes and coughed.

"Isn't he the cutest?"

"Cute? He's wet!"

"Really? I didn't know that, honest," I said, embarrassed. So I zoomed all over the house in search of a diaper, scared I was gonna flub-up Bennie's care, but also wanting to impress the doctor. What if he didn't want me to stay at the clinic? Even if C.W. and Ruth wanted it, maybe the doctor would be against it. But I tracked down an awesome wooden box and filled it up with some flannel shirts and small white towels and rags. While I was setting the stuff next to the couch, Bennie started crying and going ballistic. "Having fun yet?" I asked.

"Yea, right. I think his shirt's still dry, but let's get this diaper off."

As the doctor did his thing, I let Bennie grab my little finger. He tugged at it, mouth wide open, staring not really into my eyes but somewhere out in space. I had to giggle he was so stellar. "You want to use this towel I found for a diaper?" I asked the doctor.

"Sure, but he's definitely sick, so let's do a little exam first." The doctor laid Bennie on the couch. He asked me to get a thermometer out of the kitchen, which he put in Bennie's booty, then he checked his eyes and mouth. "Skin like porcelain. If only that could last a lifetime," he said.

"C.W. always says, Babies are a miracle that occur every day. Do you believe that?"

Dr. Merrithew shook his head. "Well, there's a baby born every day and, just like this one, most of them aren't properly cared for."

"Oh, don't say that. That's not true. Everybody loves babies. If you didn't have babies you wouldn't have Springtime or eagles or otters, just foster parents and vegetables and school and nowhere stuff like that.

You're an adult, how come you never had a baby?"

"Never wanted one, my work keeps me busy."

Dr. Merrithew put his hand behind Bennie's head, then continued, "I was an only child and I had a nanny—good old Elizabeth Crocker."

"Did you ever get, like, bored with nobody to play with?"

"When the time came—at the Academy—I had plenty of kids to play with. My parents were both professional people. Father, he was a scientist—a lab physicist—and my mother, before she started flitting and flirting and boozing around doing nothing, an ad executive. But there was a divorce and . . . it got complicated."

"C.W. says—"

"Would you stop mentioning that man, Christina," the doctor insisted, keeping his eye on the baby. "He's mad, and the sooner you realize it, the better."

What he said was ice cold, so I kept quiet. He was wrong about babies and wrong about C.W., but how was I supposed to argue with a doctor?

"Let's see what we got," Dr. Merrithew said. He pulled the thermometer and checked it. "He's got a bad fever. And his cough is very dry, like he might have something more than just a common cold. Let's get him wrapped up. He needs nourishment and Tylenol drops every four hours."

"But it's nothing serious, is it?"

"I don't know, Christina. We just have to keep a close watch and see how colicky he gets." The doctor folded a towel into a triangle and put it under his skinny booty and tucked it in on the sides. "Put those shirts over him," he said, touching the baby's cheek. "That should do."

There was a knock at the front door, so I got up and let Ruth in. She was carrying a bunch of things and I helped her put them on the kitchen table.

"How is the little blessing?" she asked.

"Quite ill, if the truth be known," the doctor said.

"Well, maybe I can help. Christina, you're wanted back at the community meeting."

"Really? I can't stay here with the baby?" I pleaded.

"I don't know. I was told you have to go to the main building and talk to Peter."

Maybe C.W. never told Trajan I was supposed to stay at the clinic like he said he would. I was hoping the doctor would pick up on my worry, but he didn't say squat. Sizing up the situation, I could see the writing on the wall real clear; the old lady was gonna take care of Bennie now, and, of course, having mother experience, she could do it better than idiot me. I looked at Bennie, wishing him love, then moved over to the door.

"Young lady, you be sure to come back later, hear me?" Ruth said.

I just split without saying a word.

RUTH

Keeping men and babies close was always a bit like mixing oil and water. The baby, being a baby, couldn't communicate correctly, and the man, not being a woman, couldn't either. That was just the Lord's way, I guess. Why, you couldn't trust my Walter with a baby if your life depended on it. He was the sweetest man in the world, but his big hands were best suited for gripping steering wheels or wrenches or maybe a beer can, but not a living thing. I heard the same from all the women folk.

But for some reason Dr. Merrithew didn't fit the mold, which surprised me. After Christina left last night, he started right in caring for Bennie. He fed the little bundle of joy some soup, changed his diaper again, and couldn't stop cradling him or massaging his arms and legs. Bennie was so relaxed he stopped coughing and fell fast asleep before you could say John Henry.

This morning the same thing happened. I slept in later than I should have, but after my prayers I checked the baby, and, lo and behold, there was the doctor down on the floor playing with Bennie. They were having a grand old time. And best of all, he'd rigged up a little frame from coat hangers with little doodads hanging from it, something to keep the baby entertained.

"The little hoodlum was up all night," the doctor reported from his horizontal position, his head resting on his hands.

"Really? I'm sorry I was no help," I said, embarrassed that I'd missed his cries and my maternal duties. "I was so tired I must have slept right through it."

"I let him suck my pinkie for nourishment. That kept him quiet."

I laughed because I'd never used that trick before.

"I like that little play set," I said.

"Just a little diversion. It's boring up here in the mountains."

"Here, let me take him now," I told the doctor.

"You sure?" he asked.

"Quite."

He lifted Bennie up and I took him in my arms.

The doctor scooted over and pulled himself back up onto the couch. I walked the baby around the house for a few minutes, stretching my limbs and staring at his little cherub face, his kinky hair and dark brown eyes. From the kitchen, I asked the doctor, "How did it feel to be a papa for a night?" I got no answer, and when I peeked into the living room, I saw the poor dear had fallen fast asleep.

Bennie was still dry, so I sat down at the kitchen table, right in the middle of a shaft of sunlight, looking out into the forest behind the house. This was the kind of view I'd always wanted, something peaceful and easy on the eyes, not the view of Smooth Auto Body we'd had in Circleville. Down the hillside the blue sky peeked between the trunks of the massive trees where the island dropped off into the canyon. Alone, blessed to be alone. Warm tingling spread over the morning goose bumps on my skin.

Bennie kicked a little bit, then cooed low like a bird. It had been so long since I'd held a youngin, I'd forgotten the beauty of it (Oh, Billy, good son, don't get me thinking of you). This is what the Virgin Mary must have felt like with baby Jesus. But, Lord Almighty, look at those liver spots on my hands. Why, next to Bennie's pure skin, my skin looked like an oatmeal and raisin cookie.

I turned and looked through the kitchen door, out the front living room window. Plentiful was quiet and just waking up. A few people wandered up the Boardwalk, going about their chores. It was like everything was normal and we were a little town down in the valley, waking up from a deep sleep with other sleepy towns around us. Was it also, as I feared, just a dream? And why was it so hard to find peace and happiness in the world? Every Sunday in church we talked about it, and now we'd come to this strange place in the mountains to talk about it. Change, a new Christian beginning, equality and justice, safe neighborhoods, jobs and progress, that's what got preached, but what did we have to show for it? Not much of anything really. Oh, I still believed and prayed that love and understanding would prevail, but when did things change from talk to reality? At this old forgotten mine?

I turned back and gazed into the trees again.

I thought about C.W. at the Resource Hour the previous evening. He'd started using the word utopia a lot. Utopia this, utopia that. We would be establishing a "utopia" here, and because of our hard work, our example would spread down to the valley and beyond. He went on and on about it, ignoring everyone's questions about practical things and the fact that someone had heard helicopters up above. A couple of people even tried to walk out, but the guardians stopped them. That was the first time that had ever happened. But C.W. didn't even seem to notice, and just waved his arms around, staring at the floor or up in the air. His behavior bothered me—it just wasn't a polite Christian-like way of addressing the needs of the congregation.

But I put all that out of mind. It really didn't make any difference now anyway; I just wanted a place to lay down and die in peace. I knew my fate was in the Lord's hands and any answers I might receive would come from Him. So, I let the doctor sleep for a good while and just held Bennie and prayed.

Word must have gotten out where Bennie was staying, because Kenny Wayne showed up at the house with breakfast provisions (two bananas), but he made so much noise that both the baby and doctor were awake by the time he left. Then, not much later, Christina brought some crackers and powdered milk. I asked her what had happened the previous night, but she just ignored me, and, instead, walked around with the baby, beaming with affection. I now understood that with her big heart, she was a born mother for sure. It was strange how lonely daughters became the good mothers they never had.

"You know, at the Morning Glory meeting, Trajan told everyone that the clinic was opening this afternoon," Christina reported, "and that if anyone needed to see a doctor to be sure to make an appointment." Her announcement got a good laugh out of the doctor from his cozy spot on the couch, and I asked her if she'd heard right: this afternoon? She whispered some tender words to Bennie, then put him down. "You got it," she answered before playfully running out the door.

I think the news about the clinic opening was a thorn in the doctor's side, because he fitfully tossed and turned for fifteen minutes, then, with great effort, sat up.

"I have never been so exhausted," he said, as much to himself as to me. He stood up and silently tested his leg.

"How's it feeling?" I asked.

"In clinical terms, exquisite with pain."

He stretched his neck and back, then, as best he could, leaned against the wall to loosen up a bit. He asked me to get some more Codeine from the kitchen pharmacy, which I did promptly, giving him some water to wash it down with. Standing in the middle of the living room, staring outside, he said he was restless being penned up in the house and wanted to get out in the fresh air.

"OK, but we can't be long if we're going to be properly prepared."

"You're the boss, Ruth, whatever you say," he said, cynical as can be.

So, while the doctor got the wheelchair set up by the front gate, I bundled Bennie up as best I could, then went outside and put him in the doctor's lap. The doctor suggested we check the westerly view, so, with a guardian pushing, we set off.

As we passed the open doors of the main building, you could hear a din of voices inside. The brethren must have still been lolly-gagging about, even though it was a good hour after the morning activities. Maybe it was my imagination, but as food dwindled and stomachs started grumbling, less and less seemed to get accomplished in the community. Moving beyond the main building, the gondola came into view on our left.

"Isn't that Bosco?" Dr. Merrithew asked.

"Where?" I asked, my eyes not good enough to see what he was talking about.

"Up on the platform."

The doctor motioned over his shoulder to the guardian. "Let's go over there," he said curiously. As we moved closer, I could see Bosco moving stores back and forth from the gondola to the engine room, but then a guardian from the back entrance of the main building approached us.

"Where you think your going?" he asked. He was just some young freckle-faced kid.

"Just talking with a friend," the doctor answered.

The young man looked at his compatriot pushing the doctor, then said, "You can't come near the cable, you know the rules."

"Wait a second," the doctor objected. "I'm the physician who's starting the medical clinic. That man up there is one of our staff." Then he yelled out, "Bosco!" He turned our way and waved, but the guardian, who had some fancy rifle slung over his shoulder, stepped in front of us. He brought the weapon down and pressed it to his chest.

"Calm down, good Christian," I said quietly, "we don't mean you any harm."

"I'll take it easy, lady, when you get your tails outta here."

As we turned around to leave, the doctor yelled out to Bosco again, telling him the clinic was opening and that we needed his help, and Bosco called back that he'd be coming shortly. As we retraced our steps, the doctor insisted on staying outside a little longer (why he was suddenly being so outdoorsy, I had no idea). I'd taken a constitutional around the perimeter of the island, and knew that on the far side of the field, near the collection of old equipment, the view was quite spectacular, so we decided to stroll over there.

The clouds charged across the sky, wonderfully white and billowy, transforming from one shape to another. Did they have a message for me, brought down from on high? I wondered. I just knew the Lord had something in store for me, something more than just the coming winter.

"Stop here where it's sunny," Dr. Merrithew told the guardian, who came to a halt.

"Look," I pointed down through the trees. Far below, in the floor of the canyon, you could glimpse a river winding off into the distance.

"Do you know the name of that river?"

"No, haven't a clue," I answered.

Bennie started coughing and kicking, so the doctor unwrapped his blanket and stood him up in his lap. His face was red, his nose running something terrible. I stepped over and cleaned him up.

"Do you want me to hold him?" I asked.

"No, I'm fine," the doctor said.

"Look at those squirrels," I said happily, watching the frisky pair chase each other up and down the long metal cylinders. "Those tanks there—C.W. said they're filled with gas. I don't know how he found out about it, but he did. He was having problems breathing and thought there might be toxins leaking out of them. He's afraid we're all going to be contaminated."

Dr. Merrithew just stared at Bennie, little flames of anger in his eyes at the mention of C.W.

"God has created so many sweet little creatures, hasn't He," I said. "What do you think of that little monkey you're holding?"

"Well, the level of a baby's helplessness astounds me."

"Do you have a family?" I asked, just to make conversation.

"I'm married, but we don't have kids."

Well, that explained it right there. Children gave a person roots

101

in the world and faith in innocent ways, something the doctor didn't seem to have a surplus of. Without the love that youngsters bring into the human heart every minute of every day, the world was a cold, miserable place. I knew because I'd known both sides of life, with, and without, family.

"You planning any?" I asked, trying to catch his eye. He gave an odd smile, then just closed his eyes and turned his face up to the sun without answering. But I just kept on, "Raising a family, it's just like worshipping the Lord, you have to give yourself up to a greater need. When my son was killed in the Day-Glo fire—"

This grabbed the doctor's attention. "The fire—when was that? Kenny Wayne also mentioned it."

My word, I thought the man lived in Quinikut County and had never heard of the Day-Glo Apartments disaster?

"That's basically what brought all these people up here—the outrage over what happened.

The Day-Glo Apartments was housing for the poor in Circleville. They used to call it Assignment 52 housing or some other fancy name, but my generation just used the word poor, dirt poor, to describe those miserable abodes. But about five months ago the apartments burned down under suspicious circumstances, killing 67 local folks. One of them was my Billy—" I stopped because I was getting soft thinking of my boy.

The doctor opened his eyes and looked at me. "This is all news to me, I had no idea," he said.

I got control of myself and continued, "Well, the corporations wanted the site of the apartments for business development—some sort of chemical production place right along the Parquat—and they'd been battling the community over the acreage for years. So, when the fire occurred everyone knew who'd set it, who was guilty of the crime."

"Did the authorities ever catch who did it?"

"Catch a powerful businessman or a politician? You may as well catch your own shadow," I said, finding myself annoyed with the silly doctor, who I figured must live with his head deep in a barrel of sand. "No, nobody was caught, but people knew what happened and took things into their own hands. You simply can't imagine. There were demonstrations, more violence—it was a terrible time. But, you see, C.W. was at the center of it. He set up a tent where the apartments had been and protested putting anything there but new housing. That crazy tent got torn down the very first night, but by the next day he'd put up a new one, and he started going through this ritual of every day putting his tent back up after it was destroyed by the authorities, and in no time the radio and television and even that Internet picked up on the story and the Day-Glo killings got all this publicity, all because of C.W.

To make a long story short, his actions started a whole Christian rebellion in Circleville and, well, here we are."

The doctor shifted in his seat, putting Bennie up to his shoulder and patting him on the back. "C.W.—he's a criminal," he said, like he was giving some diagnosis.

"No, he isn't. See, being from the favored side of the river, you just don't understand. C.W. helped us keep our pride, our hope, helped us believe in the future. Why, we're all criminals, Dr. Merrithew, until we're blessed with the Word. Take yourself, are you blessed?"

"Ruth, I don't understand your frame of reference—"

"I know you don't, because the thinking of believers and non-believers is as different as apples and coconuts. But anything is possible with faith, Dr. Merrithew, anything. That's what C.W. understands now and that's why—"

I stopped talking, distracted by a whistling sound. There it was again, a sharp whistle this time. Again, my eyes failed me and I couldn't see who it was.

"What is that?" I asked.

"It's Pribble," the doctor said. "It looks like we've been discovered. Let's go back."

We returned to the clinic, but Pribble was nowhere to be seen. Then, when we started putting Bennie down in his crib, the kitchen door opened a crack and Pribble peeked out.

"Doc, come here," he said, quick as lightning.

"What is it, Pribble?"

"Man, get in here! I got it!"

What was this strange man up to?

"Ruth, excuse me," the doctor said, putting his hand on my shoulder. "I'll be a few minutes. Don't disturb me."

BARBARA

"The phone is being a nuisance—I'll call you right back. About Face Institute for Cosmetic and Reconstructive Surgery, Barbara Eastwood speaking?"

"Barb?"

"Yes, who's calling?"

"It's me."

"Doctor, where are you?" I asked, startled. The connection went out for a second, hit by static. Charlene, the aesthetician, was passing by my door and I waved at her, pointing to the receiver, saying with my lips, It's him. She stepped into my office and waited.

"Can you hear me?" he said clearly now. "I'm on a cell phone."

"Yes, it's fine. I've cancelled a slew of patients, when are you—"

"Barbara, stop," he demanded. "Do I have your full attention?" I knew that tone of voice meant business, so I sat up straight and grabbed a pad and pencil, but, still, I hated it when he just cut me off like that.

"OK, I'm listening," I said, drawing a thick black line across the page.

"There's been an emergency. I've been kidnapped."

Kidnapped? He was always pulling pranks on me and I wasn't going to fall for this one. "Right, captured by some beautiful executive?" I asked, not unimpressed by my quick response. But as he spoke (how could I have forgotten?) I remembered the events of the week.

"The Path of Peace sect?" I cried. "Please—no!"

"I don't have a name. I got picked up on the road while I was cycling and now they have me up in the Browns."

Was this really happening? He sounded a million miles away!

"Well, they practically pillaged Falmouth and some security—"

"Listen up! You have to save me, so notify the authorities."

"Of course, I'll call immediately. Do you know where you are?" I asked, grabbing my coffee. I took a quick sip, and, yes, as expected, my hand was shaking like a leaf.

"I was told it's the old Byzantium Steel Works mine. Got it? B-y-z-a-n-t-i-u-m Steel. I'd guess it's about two hours from Circeville, out in the middle of a canyon. But the whole group is armed and violent."

"My God, are—"

"Be quiet—what happened with Magliori?"

"Well, she's arrived from Italy. I was unsure what to do, so I just kept it on hold. It sounds like I should cancel the whole thing."

There was silence. Darn it, I thought, I have to make the right decision for him! "Maybe one of the partners could handle it?" I suggested.

"No, absolutely not. Keep Bill and Sadiq out of this. If I could get out of here, there's still enough time to meet her on Thursday. Call her representative. Tell them I'm sick, no, wait . . ."

In the whole eight years I'd worked at the Institute, I don't think I'd ever waited for Dr. Merrithew to formulate a needed response, not once.

"Barb?"

"Yes, I'm here."

"Make some excuse. Say I'm performing another important surgery, say it's taken longer than expected."

"Yes. OK."

"—say I'm still absolutely committed to doing the job and that we'll know day-by-day. See what the manager says."

"Alright, I got it. Listen, Estelle phoned this morning."

"What about?"

"Well, maybe I shouldn't have, but I told her I didn't know where you were. She made some comment about you being out somewhere celebrating, whatever that meant."

"Is she still in Chicago?"

"Yes, but she had a different number."

"Say it to me."

"Just a sec. How much time do you have?"

"I don't know, so be quick."

OK, come on, where is it? I could tear this Blackberry apart—it's so confusing. He's going to think I'm an idiot if I don't have it at my fingertips—bingo!

"Here it is: 324-788-9022. Did you get that?"

"Yea. Listen, I'll call Estelle. If you talk with her, tell her I'll call her. Don't say anything about this fiasco."

"Oh, Dr. Merrithew, come on, she'd kill me—"

"Barb, I'll talk to her, got it? You don't—"

And, boom, just like that, the line went dead before I could say anything more.

I lay the phone on the desk then stood up and paced in a circle around my cubicle.

Charlene stepped in front of me. "What happened? What did he say?" she asked. I was speechless. I sat down again and put my face in my hands and burst into tears.

ESTELLE

The little things you see when you're ground to a halt—motionless. Tall tales told in the wallpaper. Perilous journeys across a painted surface. Collapsed citadels of food in plastic worlds. Raindrop intestines.

The storms are so different here. Clouds and lightning coming low off the lake, clenching the Loop in a tight gloom. Yes, the wind wins in a knockout punch, slapping the hospital silly, leaving another audience of raindrops hanging on the window, each enjoying a privileged view of hapless me and my roommate beyond the curtain.

There are buttons to push: large and red for Attention, tiny and hard-to-find for Pain Relief. But why either? Motionless is just fine. Just fine.

So much water everywhere, but no water in me. No, no breakers now. Why, when every child did it so easily, could I never learn to swim? Swimming could have taken me down the river and out to sea, then into blissful pitch black, face to face with strange undiscovered creatures, away from all the stupidity skimming the surface. But no, it was impossible to enter that liquid—it felt like cool slime—without hugging Mother's neck or hiding under a bench or in the trees or behind the cabin, avoiding my friends and . . . and summer itself. Maybe I've always been motionless, and motionless things aren't meant for the water. They prefer umbrellas instead—

"Hello. Estelle, are you awake?"

I left the water for the voice. It was my sister, Sophie. I smiled weakly.

"I'm back," she said, leaning over and pushing the hair out of my eyes.

I didn't know Fifi had left.

"How are you, sis? I couldn't tell from the look on your face whether you were sleeping or not."

"Just watching the rain," I said.

"Listen to me—you have a call."

Our eyes met.

"It's Collin."

Some match was lite in the darkness of my mind when I heard his name, but the flame didn't illuminate much.

"Do you want to talk to him?" she asked. "I read him the riot act about not being here, but, like always, he complained about his own agenda."

I thought of sitting up, but, no, I'd be shot through with uterine pain, so I just stayed on my side, rolled up like a cocoon. I put my hand out for the cell phone.

"You sure?" Sophie asked.

I nodded and gestured emphatically, she handed it to me.

"Hello," I murmured.

"Estelle, it's me."

This man. He used to swim innumerable laps in the pool, back and forth, back and forth.

"Hello? Estelle, it's me, are you there?"

"Yes."

"How are you? Are you OK? You sound groggy."

What was he assuming had happened? Could he feel the vacuum in my womb?

"Well, I won't even get into what's been happening to me, you'll find out soon enough. But I wanted to hear how you were doing and how it went."

Adventures. Making it to the sea would have been an adventure, but why no call from the deep for me? Why no evolution for me?

"Estelle, can you talk to me? The procedure must have—"

"What procedure?"

I wanted specifics, straight from his mouth. It seemed so strange to hear his diplomacy.

"I'm confused here," he said, "If this is a bad time to talk—"

"I'm listening to you instead. You mentioned a procedure. Tell me about it."

There was silence. I just couldn't give him the satisfaction of knowing.

"Collin, we'll just have to wait and see, won't we? The world's drenched and nothing's decided."

"Estelle, listen, I don't have much time here. You're not making sense and it worries me. Maybe I should talk with Sophie about what's happened."

I was waiting for that word "time". No time. Well, my clock said it was time.

"Sorry, she's watching the storm with me. Bye-bye."

CHRISTINA

After our new kitchen boss, Shawnte, stopped crushing on every little detail, we finally finished cleanup. Even though I was tired with a capital T, I quickly headed back to the clinic with another bag of goodies I'd secretly put together for Bennie and the doctor, feeling like I was sneaking away from Kenyatta Koffee again!

When I came up to the house, Pribble came bursting out the front door. "Hey, what's up?" I called out, but it was like I was covered with invisible ink. He crashed through the gate and ran off down the Boardwalk towards the cliffs. What's his prob? He didn't even wave, the jerk.

Everything was real quiet inside the house. Dr. Merrithew was sitting on the couch, checking out the wall. Ever since he lost his hair it seemed like he'd started staring at things a lot more; he looked weird and acted all convoluted. I was happy Ruth wasn't hanging around. She was probably in the bedroom praying.

"Hi," I said to Dr. Merrithew. "I brought you a double latte with cinnamon on top! No, only kidding. But I did bring some little goodies."

The doctor rubbed his smooth dome.

"Coffee, wouldn't that be nice," he said.

"Did you see Pribble?" I asked.

"Yes, he was here for awhile."

"Out front just now, he was all freaked out."

"He's always freaked out."

I set the bag on the table in front of the couch, then checked Bennie. He was fast asleep. He looked smaller than ever with his short, fat arms folded across his chest. Hello, hello, you little munchkin, I whispered, are you resting good? And, as if he heard my words, he woke up, eyes twinkling like stars, and it made me laugh. Dr. Merrithew scooted down onto the floor next to me. I looked away, expecting him to touch me, but he didn't. Was I beautiful to him, beautiful just like all the other men thought I was? I couldn't tell.

He ran his finger along Bennie's cheek.

"Where's the mobile?" he asked.

"The what?"

"The mobile—the one I made. It's not a car, but a toy. There it is, there in the corner." Right. I hadn't noticed the strange wire frame, but I went over and picked it up.

"What is it?" I asked, "It's getting all tangled up."

"Just hold it steady. Set it down over Bennie so he can reach up and play with it." I did just like he said. Looking at the strings and dangling things, I gushed, "That's really neat, I like it." I reached down and passed my hand through a piece of styrofoam and a cardboard triangle, trying to get Bennie to focus on the toy.

"Look," the doctor said, "His zygomaticus muscles tense when he looks right and left. Do you see that? Just above his lips, by the risorius muscles?"

I didn't get the doctor's mental gymnastics, but I did laugh again when Bennie's eyes suddenly got real big and worried-like, like he was listening to something we couldn't hear. What was it like being a doctor? I wondered. Understanding everything you see and people showing you all kinds of respect. Must be like Superman versus mere mortals.

"What a work in progress," he said about Bennie. "Beautiful, ugly, smart, stupid. Just a blank slate—an experience-devouring blank slate."

"He's far-out, no doubt about it. I know you're not going to like this, but C.W. has a saying, A baby is a flower that blooms every day, and everyone loves pretty flowers. Isn't that like what you feel with Bennie?"

"Not exactly. Bennie's not well."

"Really? Is he sick as he was?"

"Definitely. His fever's worse and his brown mucous speaks infection. Under normal circumstances he would go straight to the hospital."

I flicked the triangle piece again. "C.W.'s probably not gonna allow that," I said.

"That's obvious—and neither would the anti-Christ, our good man, Trajan."

I blushed, thinking back about the doctor getting knocked down and skinned.

"You've been through a lot Christina. How are you coping?"

"I'm fine, I guess. I trust in God's strength, and Jesus Christ and community."

"You do, huh? Well, remember, God isn't medicine, OK. Medicine isn't some miracle, Christina, it's a practical thing. You have to ask yourself, is Bennie safe up here? I don't think he is, not for a second."

God—God and blessed Jesus Christ—would heal Bennie. And C.W—why he'd already saved the baby's life one time, which was more than the doctor could say.

"You brainwashed fools," the doctor said under his breath.

What is he tripping on? I thought angrily. I mean, damn, I knew all the questions, but not the answers. Even if the doctor was right about everything, what was I supposed to do about it? I had to do something nice. "I think Bennie's wet again. Can I change him?" I asked.

"Do whatever you want," the doctor said, moving back to his place on the couch.

He didn't like me, I knew it. I started changing the wet towel around Bennie's bootie. The diaper was soaked in pee, like a towel you'd lift out of a swimming pool or something. Yukkk! I couldn't keep it there in the living room, so I took it into the kitchen and dumped it in a waste bag. When I came back Ruth had come outta her bedroom. Her gray hair was all messed up and you could tell she'd just taken a nap; old people always looked really out of it after taking a nap. But she helped me get a new diaper on Bennie, then I showed her the bag of goodies I'd brought. I put out some Wonder Wraps, a few dried apricots, some sunflower seeds, and half-a-bag of small carrots on the table, and Ruth ate lunch while I slowly spoon-feed Bennie some instant milk and the last of the banana. After a while Kenny Wayne and Bosco showed up and polished off the rest of the food with the doctor. I hoped everybody enjoyed it, because that was pretty much all the groceries I could scrounge anywhere.

Then Ruth announced, "If we're supposed to be open for services at 2:00 pm, and C.W.'s going to be the first patient, we have to have a meeting and get things organized." So we crowded around Dr. Merrithew, official-like, waiting for directions.

But when the doctor saw all of us staring at him, he put his arms behind his head and looked at the ceiling, as if he didn't care one way or another about the clinic. He let us ask questions, and when we gave our ideas he'd just nod his head and say, "Sure, that sounds good. Do it."

That guy Bosco was real smart and full of himself. I knew he was a way-cool mechanic, but he'd also worked in a hospital before, so, being two educated wizards, he and the doctor had a lot in common. I just sat there and listened like a megadork, staring at sick Bennie and wondering where the next banana was gonna come from.

The plan for the clinic was to set up a table out by the front gate. Everybody who wanted services would have to line up on the Boardwalk first, then go to the registration table and get signed up with Ruth. She was gonna let five people at a time pass by, and they'd sit in the chairs we'd set up in the front yard and wait their turn to see the doctor. One by one, I was going to lead each patient inside the house. Bosco would take a pulse and temperature and write all the information on a piece of paper. When the doctor told me to, I would take the paper and patient into the living room where he would do his examination. For privacy, one of the guardians had taped newspaper over the windows that looked out onto the Boardwalk, although Peter, who dropped by now and then like Trajan's little watch dog, told us the paper would have to come down every night. Bosco, who kept spouting off about presenting symptoms this and treatment plans that, had even hung up a sheet in the corner of the room so patients could take off their clothes without anybody seeing.

While all this was going on, I noticed that Kenny Wayne had disappeared. When he came back he was carrying a cardboard sign he'd made. In crayon he'd written, "Merrithew Clinic for the Sick", and under it, "Plentiful USA". That was so cool of him! And it looked really good when we hung it on the front fence.

But no sooner did the sign go up than people started gathering around, trying to get the skinny on what we were up to. There musta been 30, 40, 50 people who wanted to see the doctor! How could there be so many sick people? They musta not been saying their prayers like they were supposed to. When two o'clock hit and we were ready to rip, Ruth went out to the gate.

"All you God-fearing folks move back now. We're going to be opening in a couple minutes, but you'll need to line up single file along the street. Please be quiet and cooperate now, I'm an old lady and I can't take too much stress."

The crowd shuffled into a line then, bam, outta nowhere everybody stepped back and let Trajan through, with Peter, Shawnte, and two guardians following behind.

"You ready?" Trajan asked Ruth, his eyes fixing on me as I stood by the front door. I glanced down at my tennies, a frog suddenly stuck in my throat.

"I guess you can say that," Ruth answered. "Why are you barging in here like this was a china shop, Trajan? Wasn't there going to be a nice ribbon-cutting ceremony. That's what I heard at mealtime."

"Naw, C.W. ain't feelin too good."

"Well, that's all the more reason he should come."

"Is something not clear? He can't get out right now, granny."

"Well, I hope he's alright. Maybe we can make a house call later. I'll ask the doctor."

"You ask me, not him," Trajan said, stepping up to the table and picking up the sign-in sheet. He pretended to read it, then tossed it down.

"Peter's gonna inspect the place before you open. We need to make sure the doctor's done right by the rules."

"Well, he's really only been a part of it," Ruth said. "It's been a team effort and with God's—"

"Peter, go on in," he ordered, blowing Ruth off.

While the crowd waited, Peter walked across the yard and entered the clinic. I followed him, half-expecting Trajan to tell me to stay put. Inside, Bosco was at the table with all the medical equipment. For a sec Peter didn't know what to say, and looked around kinda lost without his big boss man.

"What's wrong?" Bosco asked.

"I gotta get some medication from you," Peter said.

"Before the clinic's opened?" Bosco asked, twirling one of his curls with his finger. "Whose it for?"

"I don't know. Trajan wants it for emergencies, I guess."

"Well, that's what we're doing here, isn't it? Dealing with emergencies."

"No comment, just following orders."

Kenny Wayne stepped out of the bedroom. He didn't say a word when he saw his brother, but just walked past him and stood in the doorway of the kitchen, folding his arms across his chest, announcing, "That's right, he's doin what he does best—following orders."

Peter moved over in front of the doctor.

"Trajan wants all your pain meds, sleep meds, and all the antibiotics you have."

"He does, does he," the doctor said. "Well, it's been my experience that what Trajan wants, Trajan gets. So, go ahead, it's in the kitchen."

"Wait a second," Bosco interrupted, walking over to the doctor. "The patients need that stuff. We have so little, there'll be nothing left for anybody."

"What do you want me to do, comrade? You go argue with Trajan and reason with his thugs about it."

Bosco waved the doctor off. "Forget it, nothing makes sense around here any more." He went back to his table and sat down, steamin.

"Can I get it now?" Peter asked.

"Sure," said the doctor.

"Well, what should I take? I don't even know what medication it is."

The doctor looked at Kenny Wayne. "Give him the Levaquin, the Codeine with Tylenol, and I think I saw some Ambien."

"You stay put, I'll get it," Kenny Wayne told his reflection. In a minute he came out of the kitchen carrying a bunch of boxes. "Here, take it. You've cleaned us out, you happy?"

"Can't you put it in something first," Peter complained.

"You put it in something," Kenny Wayne said, pushing the medicine up against his brother's chest. Then, like lightning, the boxes flew everywhere and the twins started swinging at each other.

I jumped close to Bennie to protect him, then started humming to myself. The doctor looked straight into the kitchen, not lifting a finger to stop the fight, but, thank God, Bosco jumped in to help. "Knock it off," he yelled, pulling Kenny Wayne off his brother and stepping between them. "For Christ sake, if you're gonna draw blood go out into the woods." The twins both looked down at the floor, breathing heavy, too worked up to speak or face each other.

The front door opened and Ruth stuck her head in. "Are you almost finished? We're ready to start out here."

"Give us a second," Bosco answered, "We'll be right out." After she closed the door, Bosco got a plastic bag and put the scattered boxes and packets into it, then handed it to Peter. "Get out of here," Bosco said, his voice shaking. Peter, who looked like he was about to cry, split out the front door.

Then Bosco slapped Kenny Wayne on the shoulder. "Come on, rise above it. Let's get back to our work stations."

"That's the spirit, Bosco," Dr. Merrithew teased, "heal the flock."

So, finally, the clinic officially opened, and we started leading patients through and Dr. Merrithew started doing his examinations. I was totally nervous at the start (just like when I had to learn the espresso machine at Kenyatta Koffee) and thought I was flubbing up right and left, but after awhile I got my little jobs down pat. But, wow, I had to give credit to the doctor for meeting with alotta folks. I think it was thirty-three patients when I last counted. He spent a long time with eight of the people, who I guess were really sick. A couple of patients started crying real bad and couldn't stop and had to be led away. Guardians carried one woman back to the main building who couldn't walk by herself.

But standing around, watching and listening, I got real bummed out cause everybody had so many physical problems and so many problems with their feelings and so many gripes about Plentiful, it was scary. And, of course, everyone was starving and going on about there being nothing to eat. God, I asked secretly, what are you doing up in the sky anyway? Have you forgotten about us?

❧ ❧ DOLORES ❧ ❧

It takes time but I get close to front of line now. I no really sick but I want to see Dr. Collin. No, I going to see Dr. Collin if it kill me. He my only friend now since I no talk to Uncle Ilio no more.

115

That chingadera, if we ever get off mountain my brother gonna shoot his ass.

But how to get off the mountain? How? Everywhere is soldiers with guns telling orders and everywhere there so many people be looking at me and anyway there is no trail no bridge nowhere back to Circleville. Well, Dr. Collin he smart man and maybe he know something. When he run off from that meeting (why he no walk right?) I know he doing bad.

"OK, it's your turn," a blonde girl say.

I go into yard and stand at table with old lady.

"Hello sweetheart. Now, aren't you the one who went through Initiation last night? Thank you so much for that sacrifice. Having had a fine mane of hair myself when I was younger, I know what a trauma that must have been, especially to a pretty lady like yourself."

Just shut up and forget it.

"What's your name?" she say, using a pencil.

"Dolores de la Siguenza."

"My, that name's like poetry. What's your problem today, honey?"

"My tummy no feel good?"

"Upset like with the flu, or actual pain."

"Pain like."

"Is that all?"

"Yes, that's all my pain."

"OK, sit down in that chair and wait your turn. It shouldn't be too long."

I go sit on chair with people and wait. That all I done since getting here: wait for food, wait for water, wait for bathroom. There nothing else to do. How Dr. Collin come here anyway? He have big house and fancy job and wife and he not ever talk about Christ, so why he come to this place? That just crazy. The man next to me leave so I be next in line.

I look up to trees and clouds. The air cool even though the sun it shines. Oh, how can sun shine with no being warm? How can trees be big with no plantain, no red and yellow flowers? I sad for San Salvador and sad for Father and Mama and miss my house on Avenida Hortencia and wish I never leave. Father say, Don't go, don't go, work in store, but I leave in night for Chiapas anyway. Now I see I wrong and lonely. I like to light candle at St. Perpetua's and pray to Virgin Mary for all the sins I do. So many sins I do.

The blonde girl take me in the house and I sit down with man who puts things on my arm and it blow up like balloon and he say its for my heart and I smile, OK.

Then I see Dr. Collin at other end of house and hair on arm stands up. He no see me and he just sit at a table with sheet hanging down. The blonde take me to Dr. Collin then go away. I don't know what to do so just sit and wait. Finally he look up.

"I saw you the other night. I couldn't believe it," he say and look back down. At funeral I see how Dr. Collin's hair was short but I not see this close and how changed he was from Falmouth. He have little cuts on his face like he get in night fight at bar. He pick up a piece of paper and put in box by table. He tap a pencil then look at me again.

"Well, welcome to my new clinic."

"I like. Very nice," I say for joke.

"Dolores, is anything wrong? Are you actually sick?"

"No. No sick."

I look him deep in eye, straight in eye, and he look back at me. "Well, we have a couple minutes—just talk low. How did you get here?"

"My Uncle Ilio. I don't know why I come. Stupid me. How did you?"

He wave his hand. "It's—a long story."

"Mrs. Estelle, she don't know?"

He shake his head, No. I open my eyes wide: Shit, who be with the dogs all the days?

"Dr. Collin?"

"Yes," he say, giving me little diamond eyes like he remember the sauna and rosemary cream.

"You stay here now? Plentiful—is how you pronounce it? You stay here?"

He just look at me all serious for long time.

"Why do you ask?" he finally say.

I was going to answer but the man who put balloon on my

arm he walk up and give Dr. Collin a paper. He got wild hair like wire sticking out all over. "That's the blood pressure reading for this next guy," he say. "It's very, very high for some reason."

"Alright, but I still need a couple minutes here with this young lady, so just have him wait."

"Will do—and maybe we can talk at the end of the shift, how's that sound?" Then doctor he nod his head, Yes, as the man go back.

"Why that thing?" I say pointing at the white sheet hanging.

"That's the changing room. If I need to examine a patient they can go behind there and be private."

I don't know what I think but I stand and pull sheet back and go behind. All alone I look right at Dr. Collin. He see me so I put hands under titties and open mouth and show little tongue. I smile and show pretty teeth. He look around the house, then stand up having hard time. Going slow he come over behind the sheet.

He fall into my arms and kiss me with tongue his body shaking. I kiss back and push hips into him. He feel so different with no hair and me the same. We kiss and kiss and kiss then he pull back and look in my eyes. I scratch his back with fingernails.

OK, this is time now.

"Dr. Collin, please, if you go you take me, OK? I no like it here and no way I want to stay here."

"Just touch me," he say.

I kiss again and lick lips and whisper, "I miss Dr. Collin. You have me anytime. You take me if you go, please, please, then I clean house real good."

SHAWNTE

Heaven help me, look at all these hungry faces, and nothing prepared but my leftover soup from lunch; no settings out, no cider to drink, just bare tables. If this place was a real soul food restaurant, we wouldn't be making a dime.

I stepped behind the curtain and started addressing my new crew.

"Y'all gotta get your dogs in gear now, hear me?" I said to anybody who'd listen.

"Get that stinky trash outside before I faint," I said to one helper.

Another guy walked by with a plastic bowl filled with utensils. "Just use spoons," I said. "Save the rest."

We were dirtying up everything we had, then it just sat round in piles because we didn't have proper water for cleaning. You can wipe things clean only so many times before they just stay dirty. In the meetings with Trajan, he kept beating the same drum, discipline, discipline, discipline, but damn, we needed a ton and only had an ounce, if that. I wanted to astound the congregation with my cooking and some new recipes, but what credit I be getting for cheese spread and pickles on crackers, or Cherrios as filling in the Wonder Wraps, or more brown rice with soy sauce?

I checked Christina. She was dumping out the last of the canned corned beef.

"Girl, you waiting to score with no seconds on the clock? Come on, hurry up, people's stomachs be broadcasting."

She didn't say anything, the bitch, keeping at her own pace.

"Did you hear me?"

"Sure—you're yelling right in my ear," she answered, turning her back to me.

What, I asked myself, am I gonna do with an attitude like that? I had a mind to put her straight in my sights, but, following Trajan's lead, I kept my cool, waiting patiently for the wind to change in my direction.

I knelt down and started tearing the top off a box of cups, when the holy man, Charles, stepped behind the curtain. Like always (I knew it was our common flavor) he ignored me.

"Greetings, Christina!"

The girl looked up, but didn't make a peep.

"I haven't talked with you in ages. The Lord has me running too many errands, I guess," he said, winking his eye. "How's the baby child?"

"OK. He's coming later with Ruth. We got word to bring him along."

"Good. We have some new music for tonight. We've been able to do some practicing with the group you saw yesterday."

"That's nice. Did you forget to invite me?"

I just had to break this session up.

"Charles, please, we're on the clock here. This here is my worker and I need her doing just that."

Christina looked up at me. "Get real—I'm not your worker. I work at the medical clinic and I volunteer here."

"Whatever crown you wanna wear is fine—"

Charles interrupted. "Shawnte please, give me a moment." He knelt down next to the girl, but before he could utter a word, she started in complaining: "Who's gonna memorize it, Charles? Who? I bet none of them even know what The Melopedia is."

"I know what you're saying, I do. You always sing the songs before anyone. But C.W. knows your hands are full with the baby. Come on, I mean just because other hummingbirds learn to fly too doesn't mean C.W.'s words and melodies won't live on in your heart. They always will, so no hard feelings, OK? Now, we've set up a special chair on the stage for you and the Blessed One, so after you're done in the kitchen, please come join us. Do it as a special favor to me."

The girl nodded, sparks still flying from her nostrils, then Charles left.

With all that over with, I got the crew down to a good fast grind. We got the table settings put out. The big container of soup finally got bubblin on the gas stove and bowls went out six to a table. So did the platters of canned corned beef and my new cracker creation. There was even some mixed nut stuff we served, but for some reason, and I was going to investigate this, all the dried fruit and carrots had disappeared. But as I leaned against the back wall and chewed on some raisins, I could tell things weren't right. I mean, when you're a real cook there comes that moment of achievement when your work is done and you serve up what you've created, then, with everybody busy eating and drinking, talking and laughing, you know you done right by satisfying people's needs. But checking out the room, there was no satisfaction to be found anywhere, just tired, disappointed eyes asking, Is this all there is?

I noticed the medicine man and his staff had settled at the same table down by the stage, except with a little more guardian coverage this time. Ruth, who'd been nowhere to be seen in the kitchen lately, was handing the baby over to Christina, who seemed to shine like the sun holding that little one. Christina trailed Charles up onto the stage and sat down in a chair. Since there was so little food, the meal (the snack?) was over in no time and the guards shut the back doors. Trajan didn't want anyone running off like yesterday.

Charles immediately pulled out his Bible and started reading from Deuteronomy, doing his best to quiet everybody down. He went on and on about Moses hiking to the plains of Moab, near the city of Jericho, traveling all across the land that the Lord had promised to Abraham. When Moses passed away, all the people lamented and cried for thirty days, then Joshua took Moses' place in the tribe and a new generation was born.

God knows I believed in Heaven and Hell, but until someone threw dirt on my cold face, I was just gonna keep my ear to the street and ignore that ancient history stuff. And it seemed like a lot of people around me felt the same way, because nobody seemed to be paying much attention to Charles' sacred routine. The crowd musta been waiting for the brass to show.

But Charles kept working the room, flashing his smile and jivin about Joshua coming aboard, until his act got rudely interrupted when Bennie started crying. Why, that brat wailed something fierce. Charles waited politely for the baby to quiet down, but the little guy kept on with his verbal nourishment.

"Mm, mm, mm, there's nothing better than the sound of a baby crying," Charles said happily. "That's nature's greatest symphony right there, a melody that keeps the wolves at bay." He walked over and stood next to the girl. "Go ahead, young man, speak your piece, don't mind me." And Bennie did just that, spitting his lungs again. Charles, making the best of a bad situation, gave the crowd a bothered look, shaking his head, getting the people to laugh.

Then there was a banging at the rear entrance and guardians pushed open the tall doors. For a second nothing happened, then a man was pushed through. His hands were bound behind his back and his mouth was taped shut. Why, it was Pribble, the driver man who's always hanging on the outskirts of things. But, Lord Almighty, he looks bugged out with fear.

Then Trajan came through the doors too. He was scowling, looking tough as nails, and when he pointed down to the stage, the guardians moved the man along. Marching down the aisle, Trajan grabbed a loose chair, and, when they all got in front of the stage, he had the guards sit the man down on it. Alone on his lonely throne, the poor guy just hung his head helplessly.

Everyone was wondering, What is going on? So I got off the wall and stepped up closer to hear better. As Trajan walked up onto the stage you could hear a pin drop. Of course, Charles tried to make the best of things.

"Trajan, good evening, and God bless," he said, trying to hide his surprise at the rude entrance. Trajan didn't say anything, so Charles went on, "We were just speaking about the death of Moses and were about to hear from the new chorus."

Trajan shook his head, then said, "Well, we got something else to talk about now."

Charles nodded. "OK. Is C.W making an appearance to-night?" he asked, glancing at the audience.

"Naw, he's not," Trajan said, his voice all nervous, like he was about to wet his pants. Boy, you better lock your image down right now or your gonna lose your street cred forever. Trajan walked over to the edge of the stage, right above the prisoner man. This is your moment of truth, baby, show me how right I been.

"C.W.'s busy. But he told me, Trajan, since you're my right hand man, you go lead the meeting. So that's what I'm doing. I accepted the offer cause there's always a first time for everything."

He kept looking at the prisoner. "The thing is, we're in danger—but first I'm gonna talk about Pribble Sebastian-Coe. You all should know that this guy tattled on us. C.W., he's got this cell phone nobody knows about. It's for emergencies, but Sebastian-Coe here, he stole it and used it." I thought for a moment Trajan was gonna kick the man in the head, but he continued talking. "He called down to Falmouth and spilled the beans, told the authorities about where we are, about the mountains, about Plentiful, and—well, you all heard it, I know I did—there was the sound of helicopters this morning. Helicopters! You know what that means?

Traitor, squealing pig, Judas, whatever—this guy right here, excuse my language, why he just fucked us over, that's what he did."

Charles put his hand to his head, shocked by the funky language, then he stood up tall and gestured with friendly hands. "Trajan, we all share your concern about the helicopters, that, and our general well-being. But the laity also knows who Pribble is. He's just a simple man—"

"Stay out of this, Charles. He's gonna be punished. There's nothin dirtier than what he did, so right here in front of everybody, right in front of God, he's gonna get what's coming to him.

All of you, you see Sebastian-Coe? Well, you're gonna to see him a lot closer. Helpers? Let's go, bring the stuff out."

Some guys came round the side of the stage, each carrying a box. It was clear they were from the Gardens, what with their black sneakers and t-shirts with the sleeves cut off. As the five dudes lined up next to the prisoner, chants started going out from the far side of the building, "Creigh-ton, Creigh-ton, Creigh-ton—", but Trajan cut the voices short with a wave of the hand.

"Not much is gonna change here at Plentiful, nothin except the colors we wear. You see this orange scarf I got around my neck? It means I'm from Creighton Gardens, near the Plimski Market and the Geo Delicatessen, not uptown, not the Peaks or the river, and, you know what, I'm proud of that. We all know the five neighborhoods—that's who we are, right? So it's time we get proud of who's from where, and who has what roots. That way we can organize ourselves and get shit done.

So everyone come up now and get yourself a bandana—and make sure it's the right color, and make sure you wear it all the time from here on out. Go by neighborhood, starting right here with the Starr Road gang. And when you come up, look at Pribble here. Look him right between the eyes and decide what his second punishment should be."

Everybody kinda stared at each other, not knowing what to do. You could tell the whole community was crazy-lost without C.W., but people were also standing up and obeying Trajan's orders too! So, one by one, people started getting outfitted with neck wear—the Starr Road gang (purple), Creighton Gardens (orange), the Peaks (yellow), Riverside (green—that be me!), and Pope Street (red)—then checking the sorry man. It went on for maybe twenty or thirty minutes.

When people finally got back to their seats, Trajan announced, "Now that looks good, real good. Some identity, that's what we got. Charles, go on doing what you were doing." Then Trajan stood off to the side of the stage, folding his arms, looking relieved. Well, I'll be, I proudly thought, he'd done the heavyweight thing and brought on his best noise, no doubt about it. Now I was more convinced than ever I was in the right orbit.

With Pribble still wearing his dunce cap, Charles announced that some new music was gonna be played. That same group came up onto the stage, all flashing new colors. After a little guitar and water bottle introduction, the red-haired woman with the killer voice started singing from on high:

Our scout has returned
The hawk with the infinite gaze
He flew to the stars
Swooped down over the cities
And on his secret watch
Looked into enemy eyes.
Now he is perched on our shoulder
And the message he brings,
Circle the wagons, circle the wagons
Circle the wagons or be buried deep.
Buried deep
Without love without hope
Buried deep
Without bread without wine
A new generation
Left to drink poison from the wishing well.

There's a time to spread like a flood across the land
To nourish the infant seeds.
There's a time for digging the golden earth
To feed the family you love.
But when dreams have been looted
Your wheels broken down
The road too rutted too rocky to move,
Circle the wagons, circle the wagons
Circle the wagons or be buried deep.
Our scout has returned
The hawk with the infinite gaze
And the message he brings,
Circle the wagons for the Lord above.

CHRISTINA

Poor Pribble, what happened to him? Just majorly messed up! I couldn't get that reality off my brain as I walked behind Ruth down the trail. Since Dr. Merrithew had felt a lot of pain using his crutches at dinner, Kenny Wayne was pushing him in the wheelchair somewhere up ahead of us. But the old lady moved soooo slow; I mean, speed prehistoric. Stopping and checking for rocks, then moving along a little bit, then admiring the hoot of an owl, then creeping a little farther, and me holding Bennie the whole time.

"Ruth, did you catch that song?" I asked, trying to get her mind off her feet. "What'd you think?"

"I enjoyed it, sweetheart. But I like any kind of music, so I'm probably not the best judge."

The song kept morphing in my brain. I'd captured all the words and could even sing it if somebody asked me, but the melody I wasn't quite sure about.

When we finally got to the headquarters there was more security than the day before. Everybody was wearing the five colors, so I knew all the guardians were Trajan's special crew. The front door was slowly unlocked and the men led us inside.

It was all dark and hard to see as we moved into the big room. After my eyes adjusted, I spotted C.W. spread out on the mattress against the back wall.

A guardian stopped Kenny Wayne and Ruth and the doctor out in the middle of the floor, but let me walk over to C.W. There were bottles all around his bed, a candle burning in each one. Shadows bounced off the ceiling.

"C.W.?" I asked.

"Who is that?"

"Christina, silly Popeye. Are you OK? Why you lyin down?"

"The marathon. Just resting from the—" But then he stopped. "Shhhhh!" he hissed, raising up on his elbows, turning his head to listen. There was a sound like a lawn mower way off in the distance.

A guardian burst through the doors. "You can see something down south. It's flashing a spot light," the man said, standing at attention.

"Thanks for the proclamation," C.W. said. "Now go tell that flying machine to leave us alone."

"But . . . OK, yea, I'll get right to it," the guardian answered, slipping out of the room. C.W. chuckled to himself, then groaned, his stomach jiggling like a bowl of Jello. "To laugh or to cry—which?" he asked himself, scratching his face real fast.

"I brought Bennie!" I said cheerfully.

"Ah, I could sense a clear vibration in the room." C.W. sat up and awkwardly stuffed a pillow behind his head. "Here, give him to me," he said.

To be true blue, I didn't really want C.W. to hold Bennie cause he seemed in a strange space, but I stepped onto the mattress anyway and handed him the baby. He raised Bennie up and his little legs went crazy kicking. "Second generation Plentiful!" C.W. said, grinning. "Dr. Merrithew? Dr. Merrithew?"

The doctor rolled himself over. "What?" he asked.

"How's the little gentleman's health?"

"He still has a serious fever and cough, despite all the top-notch clinical services."

C.W. paused for a moment, then, without really looking at

what he was doing, he put Bennie down on the mattress. "Why are the educated always so sarcastic, always spewing toxic words and contesting the Lord's poetry and logic? You learned that language on your rotations, didn't you, Doctor?

"I learned a lot of things on my rotations, C.W., but, believe me, none of it has been applied here," Dr. Merrithew answered. He breathed deeply and then folded his hands like he was super-bored, his eyes never leaving C.W.

"A lifetime of rotations . . . " C.W. mumbled.

I just stood there, kinda waiting for C.W. to do something with Bennie, but I realized that he'd just totally forgotten about him. Helpless as a turtle on its back, Bennie started to freak, so I sat down on the edge of the mattress and picked him up. I kissed his forehead and then smelled him for pooh, but realized the stink was coming from C.W.

There was a long silence, then finally C.W. started telling a story to the ceiling.

"I'm being stalked . . . Earlier today I remembered something from years back and now it's haunting me, just like some ghost. I was staying in this little attic room at my Aunt Gayle's house near Fossett Park. Good old Fossett Park, where you could always hear the organ from the merry-go-round. She was a widow, a nice old lady who'd worked her whole life as a waitress at Gugliotti's, and she let me stay at her place rent-free and I was happy to take advantage of her generosity.

But in that attic she had this little desk that I used when I had fantastic delusions of being a wage-slave and writing a column for that local rag, The Sentinel, that used to be given away on every street corner. What a gaudy dream that was, to actually be paid for writing something! But one day—you know, just innocently, like any simple fellow who was getting a stamp or a thumbtack—I opened the left-hand drawer of that desk and entered this . . . this other universe of little items and things. You know what I'm talking about: all the staplers, address books, the rubber bands, rulers, breath mints, notepads with sticky edges, hand lotion and . . . and erasers (I clearly remember a bag of brokenhearted erasers) that fill our world.

I dug deeper and deeper into the drawer, and at the bottom I found a hundred and seventeen pencils (I counted every one!), all bundled together with tape like little stacks of wood that would never, ever, find a fireplace. Shock set in . . . it's silly, but I couldn't stop looking through all the drawers. I mean, what was it all used for, these products of our fields and forests and assembly lines? Who was going to use this silly abundance? That was the point, wasn't it? Using things. But maybe not . . . and if not, then why the abundance in the first place?

I remember checking one of the pens; it still had ink. A marker made a red line. But so what? All of it was doomed for eternity to an attic drawer with no . . . praxis, no guiding hand. And none of the pencils were sharpened. Here I was, a writer struggling to produce something, anything, and none of the pencils had a point, not one!

But how it multiplies in the little prison desks of old women. That's the thing, the crime, all the crap packed into every drawer in every house in every city in this fat cat country of ours, not to mention the infinite things, beyond our wildest comprehension, ramified exponentially, in refrigerators, in garages, closets, purses, car trunks, basements. That's the crime—all the stores . . . all the stores packed away . . . stores bought from stores and stored in storage . . . storage behind stores offering stores . . . stores filled with stores stored in—"

"What about Pribble?"

The voice startled me. It was Kenny Wayne out in the middle of the room. He didn't try to move cause the guard was there, but you could tell by his nervous voice, his clenched fists, that he was fuming. "What's he being punished for?" he asked.

"Most words are just echoes of other words," C.W. said to himself, raising his head up and looking out at us for the first time since we'd arrived. "Kenny, the doctor and Pribble have been naughty boys. Isn't that right, Dr. Merrithew?"

The doctor just stared silently.

Kenny Wayne went on, "Pribble wouldn't hurt a fly, C.W., and the doctor, he said he got beat up too. Pardon my expression, but that's bullshit. It's just wrong."

"Kenny, naughty boys get punished. Evil is always revealed and brought to Judgment, Trajan has helped me understand that. See, that's the piece that's been missing for me all these years. After the moment of Inspiration, how do you maintain focus—how do you keep a believer's mind from becoming distracted by all the folly around us—while making the Final March? Well, Trajan is my instrument for that discipline now."

Kenny Wayne shuffled his feet and looked down. "Well, I'm not sure what you're talking about, but no way it's fair," he said helplessly, stepping back into the shadows.

C.W. pointed at the doctor. "Dr. Merrithew, just out of curiosity, who did you call? Who was it?"

"I called my office," the doctor replied.

"He called his office," C.W. cried out, throwing his arms up in the air. "Well, I hope you had a nice chat, but with helicopters flying about, I doubt that's—Ah, these harsh accusations pouring out of me. Let me cut out my bitter tongue."

Dr. Merrithew moved his wheelchair a little closer to the mattress, then said, "Why don't you just call off this social experiment and drive everyone back down the hill. People are suffering, C.W., and that baby is very sick."

"Raise the white flag", C.W. said, "is that the prescription? But you're floating on the surface of things, Doctor. Sure, the boards of directors, the police chiefs, the silly social workers in their death-cell offices, they'd all like a sign of surrender. They'd love to see us file back into Circleville like so many prisoners of war, then begin their evaluations. But you underestimate the power of God that guides us here. Faith in the One Truth—Jesus Christ—and social justice, that can't be found at the IMF or on the surface of Mars or in the dairy section of your local convenience store. It's in your blood, man! The truth is pumping through your veins, and that's what Plentiful is made of—pure flesh and blood."

C.W. paused, twisting his head from side to side, then continued staring up at some place on the ceiling that only he knew about. Then he did the weirdest thing: He pointed at something up there and smiled, like he was having a conversation. I felt scared suddenly and had to do something.

"How's your back, C.W. Want a massage?" I asked.

He turned his face towards me, like he never heard my question. "Bennie is flesh and blood, isn't he, Christina? We begin the March, he crosses the finish line."

I smiled at C.W., agreeing, rocking the baby in my arms. I was going to say something, but C.W. had already looked back up to that mystery spot. "Doctor, have you enjoyed being a father figure?" C.W. asked.

"I haven't been enjoying anything, C.W."

"Do you have children?"

"No, I don't."

"Neither do I. What a coincidence."

"What?"

"Two childless men."

"A rather common coincidence actually."

"Not really. Most men have children, the others, like you and I, are just haunted by their . . . poor harvest. But I have God and my beliefs. What do you have? Tell me, I'm curious."

"Sanity, C.W. My sanity."

"Yea, good old sanity. I've heard rumors about it, just like the little rumor flying around outside just now. Well, bring this sanity of yours—this Civilization with its laser gun soldiers and satellite cameras and journalists scribbling their yellow stories with lonely pencils—bring it across the cable. But don't expect anything from us but flesh-and-blood, you hear me? There will be no artifice of any kind, no artificial sweeteners, here at Plentiful, just meat on the bone, and that can't be conquered. You see, we're the most powerful living breathing people on earth, that's prophecy."

Dr. Merrithew stood up from his wheelchair and immediately the guardians against the wall got restless.

"I need to move," he explained. "I've got a cramp in my calf." He walked in a circle, using the wheelchair for support, stretching his injured leg. "C.W., I need to lie down. Are you through with us?"

C.W. let out a laugh. "Doctors are all masters of the brief, insensitive remark, and you're no different, Dr. Merrithew. But yes, I'm glad you asked because I've had something on my mind."

"I don't doubt it. What is it?" Dr. Merrithew said.

"I'm going to be staying here. I'm not going outside—not going out into the world—any longer. This mattress, this is my new pulpit."

I was confused. "You mean like every day, all the time?"

"That's right, Golden Throat."

"Well, what about all of us, what about Plentiful? We need you."

"What about? Who will? What if? How are we? What then? Pleeaaaasse! I've asked those questions a thousands times and now here I am, in these trees on a cliff. Which Shakespeare cat was that, who was hanging from a cliff? I forget. But all of you, if you have to go, go. I bid farewell to the taaaalking, taaaalking, the riddles, quandaries, the conundrums, the ethical dilemmas, the diagrammed sentences. Good-bye to the blah, blah, blah."

I couldn't understand where he was coming from. "The Golden Stories—are you just blowing that off?" I asked, frowning.

C.W. shifted his weight and raised his head with difficulty. "There are three candles that have gone out over there. If someone could please, please light them. I've got something stabbing right between my eyes."

"Whatever," I said in frustration, more angry with him than I'd ever been.

Kenny Wayne obediently walked over, knelt down, and lit the candles with some matches from his back pocket.

C.W. breathed deep and groaned again. "Doctor? Come and see me, will you?"

Dr. Merrithew just smiled like a fox. I think he knew C.W. had tipped over the edge and was easy prey. "Of course, and we can reminisce about old times," he said.

C.W. slapped the mattress with his hand, misunderstood. "No, a mirror—a mirror's what I need. Christina?"

"What?"

"The calorie count. How many calories? Tell me."

I looked around at everybody, not knowing how truthful to be. "We're doing fine, C.W. I shoulda brought you something to eat. I'm sorry."

But there was no response. I looked over and C.W. had started breathing so deep his cheeks puffed out like a frog. Realizing that he'd just crashed out on us, I stood up with Bennie and we all left the headquarters.

There was moonlight on the trail going back. The forest was totally quiet, except for the beat of our footsteps and the crickets.

What, I asked myself, had happened to my leader, my Guiding Light? He was all weirded out and that could only mean this was turning into Trajan's fortress now. No way could I deal with that concept, no, not at all, not ever, so, seeing a black spot in my mind, I let the wheels spin and drifted into it. There was no controlling it. *I looked out a window to the other buildings . . . The roofs were burning . . . Rows of people just stared back at me and waved before jumping into the red steam . . . Then me too . . . The flames licking at the glass then coming inside . . . Looking down, my legs just melted away, then my breasts and face and eyes too until nothing was left but my soul . . . But my soul escaped up into the sky . . . It flew across the valley floor . . . Out beyond the brown and yellow fields and the oceans and mountains . . . All by itself, all alone, my soul caught a ride on a spinning planet heading—*

I bumped right into Kenny Wayne and Ruth. Whoa! He'd stopped the wheelchair in the middle of the trail for some reason. I took a sec to find myself and think straight again.

"What's wrong?" Dr. Merrithew asked, his back to everyone.

Kenny Wayne stepped off the path, pointing towards a whitish color on the tree. It was throbbing back and forth, the moonlight making it sparkle.

"Be careful now, it's moving," the guardian behind me said. Kenny Wayne picked up a branch and moved towards it, but suddenly it flew right at us. I freaked and let out a scream, but the thing just dropped by the path, wings flapping slowly.

Kenny Wayne poked at it. "It's a bird," he said.

"Naw, it isn't," I said, "it's something different."

Dr. Merrithew looked over his shoulder at what we were doing. "It's a butterfly or a moth," he said before turning back.

"But look how huge it is!" Ruth said, and, yea, if I hadn't been holding Bennie I would have tried to touch it myself, it was so alien.

"Just kill it," the guardian said.

"No, don't do that!" I said angrily, looking at the stupid guy. "Why would you have to kill it?"

"It might bite you, like a bat."

"Naw, Dr. Merrithew's right," Kenny Wayne said, "it's an insect thing. But it sure is spooky. The wings are like fans—they gotta be six inches long."

The thing looked like it might try to fly again, but then it just crawled up onto the branch that Kenny Wayne was holding. It stayed perfectly still, waiting.

"Let's bring it back," Kenny Wayne said, raising it up.

"What are we gonna do with it?" I asked.

"I don't know. It can fly away if it wants to."

"Hurry up, I'm getting cold," Dr. Merrithew complained.

So the guardian took over pushing the wheelchair, and we continued up the trail to the clinic, taking the creature with us.

RUTH

Yes, finally it had come to pass. A miracle had been bestowed on the land—a blessing for this ignorant sinner. Ever since I was a little girl I'd heard stories and sermons about how God was revealed through miraculous acts. I always believed such a thing was possible and waited patiently, year after year after year, for that special moment to occur, but it never did. So, in my old age, I'd be the first to admit that my hopes had dimmed and that I was plagued with doubts about whether, despite my most devoted prayers, a sign from God's hand would ever show itself to me in this lifetime.

But now, looking out the bedroom window, I knew I was wrong. I simply hadn't believed deeply enough. Such a beautiful spectacle I'd never seen: thousands of virgin white butterflies; butterflies not of this world, but another, flying everywhere you could see. I knew this was God's special message to me. Dear Lord, thank you for unfolding your hands and blessing me.

I put my face against the window, watching, smiling, my breast brimming with wonder. The air was thick with the beauties. They landed here and there on tree stumps and covered the bark of the great trees like a blanket of mother-of-pearl. Then, boom, there was a glorious angel right above me on the window. I put my hand up to it; it kept still, welcoming me, then spread its wings, telling me its secrets. Hello messenger from a heavenly dream, I said, I've been waiting for you. Deep within my heart I knew what all this revealed. Plentiful was meant to be! Our settlement had God's blessing! Passing my last days here was going to be a divine culmination, as I'd hoped it would be. Now, somehow, all that had passed before in my life—my rocky childhood, Walter, my lost boy, the decades of work and struggle—made perfect sense. God had overlooked my doubts and forgiven my selfishness. But was the miracle for my eyes alone, or did others see it as well?

I opened the bedroom door to find out. Through the living room windows I could see the same white spectacle filling the air. Oh, Prince of Peace and Son of God, now everyone will know!

I was about to tell Dr. Merrithew and Bosco, who were still inside talking, when the front door opened and Christina peeked in.

"Ruth, I was just coming to get you. Come out here and look at this!"

"I know, dear, I saw it from the back," I said excitedly, putting my hand on the doorframe for balance, then stepping out onto the porch. Perched in the trees, bouncing through the air, settled on the bushes and rocks, the butterflies made the landscape move and breathe.

"Amazing grace," I said, putting my arm in Christina's.

"It's radical. There's thousands out there," Christina said.

"It's God's illumination."

Up and down the Boardwalk people wandered about amidst the butterflies, shouting in amazement, laughing, pointing and touching, some spinning in circles, lost in their own flights, others dancing and singing. Then I saw Peter walking back and forth in the crowd, announcing, "Everyone meet at the cliffs for a celebration! Meet at the cliffs for a celebration!"

"Well, I don't think we'll be opening the clinic as scheduled," I told Christina.

"Shoot, I guess you're right. Darn it," she said.

Looking about, I wanted to wander amidst the butterflies and just be a part of it all. Talking seemed somehow meaningless and petty. "Well, this is better medicine anyway," I said with satisfaction. "I'm going to take an adventure and go down to the cliffs. Do you want to come with me?"

"Naw, you go ahead, Ruth, I'm gonna hang here."

I gave Christina one more big hug.

"Thank you for praying. Now, after seeing this, you can understand its power and say good-bye to all your troubles."

Christina smiled. I knew she was trying to be transformed by the miracle, but how successfully was hard to tell, what with her shy eyes escaping me at every turn.

"I'll be back in a jiffy," I said. "Keep an eye on Bennie. If you change your mind, come on down."

Then I stepped out into the street, raising my hands up to the butterflies like St. Augustine to the doves.

CHRISTINA

I hurried back inside to tell Dr. Merrithew about all the stellar stuff that was happening. You woulda thought with all the noise he'd have checked it out, but no, he was still hanging with Bosco.

"What's all the fuss about?" the doctor asked.

"It's a surprise, come and see," I said, kneeling down and finding Bennie asleep in his crib.

He waved me off. "We're busy, Christina."

"No, you have to, Dr. Merrithew, you won't believe it. Bosco, you gotta come too." It took some more coaxing, but I finally got the doctor out on the porch. Bosco stayed in the doorway behind us, looking worried about something.

"See? Didn't I tell you?" I said, pointing at the butterflies.

"Would you look at that," Dr. Merrithew said, leaning up against the railing. "Must be some hatch that occurs this time of year."

"Hatch? What's that?"

"When it's a certain season, and when it gets a certain temperature, insects will appear like this. Like, people go trout fishing when the hatch is right."

"Hello, Doc," a man yelled from out on the Boardwalk, and all the people around him waved and whistled at us. Ruth was out there too, spinning through all the butterflies with a circle of women who were holding hands. Watching all the fun, I couldn't help but giggle to myself, my heart warm and golden.

But then I noticed the musicians who'd performed at Resource Hour the night before. They were walking down the middle of the street, singing "Food for the Soul." My eyes stuck like fly paper to the red-haired woman, the new diva; she was even taller than I remembered her being. I whispered the lyrics to myself as they passed by:

> *Food for the soul*
> *Where can you buy it?*
> *At your friendly co-op, not the five and dime.*
> *Pick it from the garden*
> *It's green and juicy*
> *At your friendly co-op, not the five and dime.*
> *The Lord has honey for your lips*
> *And gravy to drip from your fingertips*
> *You can taste flavors sublime*
> *At your friendly co-op, not the five and dime.*

Remembering the song made me so angry at C.W. that I dug my fingernail into my skin until it hurt. "Well, that's it, I just thought you would want to see it," I said to the doctor. Then I saw the little temporary cage that had been set up for the butterfly we'd found the previous night. The creature was lying flat on its side, a goner. I knelt down, staring at its bright pink and silver wings. "We shoulda set it free," I said.

"That's going to happen to every one of those real soon," Dr. Merrithew said from over my shoulder. "They'll probably all die in the next day or so I would think."

"What? I did not hear that, OK?" I said, scrunching my nose and making a face. "I did not hear a word of what you just said."

"I'm not kidding."

I looked out into the trees. There were so many beautiful fliers you couldn't count them all. But if every one died there'd be a carpet of them all over the island, piles of dead things everywhere you stepped. I felt like I was going to be sick; I bolted through the front door and scrambled into the bedroom, closing the door behind me.

Standing there, I had a couple dry heaves then sat down against the wall and started crying—crying like I'd never cried before. The tears just poured outta me like a bad rain. I tried to stop, but it was no use, so I just let everything turn to liquid, hugging myself and rocking back and forth, green spots bursting behind my eyes . . .

When I finally dried up, I took a couple minutes to rest and catch my breath. I felt empty as a paper bag. There was blood on my hand from my fingernail cut and I wiped it off and stood up, not wanting anyone to discover me acting so mushy and helpless. Outside, tree limbs were swaying in the wind, slapping the window, butterflies blown up against the glass. I looked away in fear and went back into the living room. I checked Bennie again. He'd rolled over on his side in the crib and, afraid something was wrong, I moved like lightning and picked him up. Jesus, thank you, I thought, he was still his happy self! I shook his little bag-of-groceries body and he burped, and the more I smiled, the more he smiled, and we ended up laughing at each other. Sweet, sweet Bennie, what's gonna happen to you?

I heard voices coming from the kitchen, so I took the baby and went to see who it was. When I opened the door, Bosco jumped back in surprise.

"What are you doing? You by yourself?" he asked, all paranoid.

"Duh, yea, what's wrong with you?"

"Nothing," he said, peeking out to the Boardwalk, then shutting the door behind me.

Dr. Merrithew was sitting at the kitchen table. "Christina, do you have a minute? I want to talk to you about something."

"Sure, I guess."

"Sit down," the doctor said, and Bosco pulled up a chair for me. Dr. Merrithew put his hands together on the table, then breathed heavily, thinking.

Here it comes, I'm gonna get kicked out of the Clinic.

"Christina, are you happy here?" the doctor asked.

"I love working here. Please don't—"

"No, not that. I mean, are you happy here in Plentiful?"

I had to think seriously about the question. Last week, I would have known for sure, but, being honest, I wasn't so sure any more.

"The lineup's changed, I admit that."

"Yes, but it's more than that, isn't it?" The doctor stared right at me. "Has Trajan hurt you?"

My face went kinda numb. Why was he asking me about that? I was being as good as I could be. I stood up real quick. "I gotta go," I said.

"Christina, sit down now, please," the doctor said. "This isn't an interrogation. I'm just concerned about you."

I did as he asked, then glanced at Bosco, who was biting a fingernail.

"There's nothin to worry about," I lied.

The doctor turned and looked out the back windows. "But I do worry about you," he said. "You, and what to do with Bennie."

I looked down at the baby boy, rubbing his fuzzy hair.

"What's going to happen to him, Christina?"

"What do you mean?"

"Here at Plentiful."

"I don't know. He got saved."

Bosco came over and sat down at the table with us. "But now the baby's going to be in the middle of a fight, isn't he?" he said.

"What are you talking about?"

"Christina, Plentiful's been discovered, do you realize that?" the doctor said. "Helicopters have been checking this spot out for days. I don't want to shock you, but do you know what's going to happen when the police, the army, whoever, come after this place. It's not going to be pretty. Unless we surrender peacefully—and you know Trajan and C.W. aren't going for that—it's going to be a war."

What he was saying was too strange to think about, so I just cuddled Bennie the best I could.

But Bosco started up again, "Do you think they know a baby is in the midst of this? No, because they view this community as a bunch of criminals—"

"OK, OK," I interrupted, "I catch your drift, jeez."

Dr. Merrithew shifted in his chair and looked straight into my eyes.

"We need to escape, Christina."

I smiled, goofy-like. Did I hear what I think I heard?

Bosco was about to say something, but Dr. Merrithew raised his hand to stop him. He smiled at me and continued, "Christina, we've been through so much together, so much in so little time. You're a total stranger, but somehow when I talk with you I feel like I'm talking to an old friend. Listen, please, we want you and Bennie to leave with us before there's some sort of tragedy here." Dr. Merrithew reached over and put his hand on my shoulder. I jerked away at first, then accepted his touch.

"Believe me, it's not like you're going to reveal where this place is hidden when you escape. They already know. You would just be saving Bennie, and that's the important thing, isn't it?" I stared at Dr. Merrithew. He knew he was right, and I knew he was right, but what could I do? He pressed my shoulder sweetly, then put his hand back on the table.

I looked into Bennie's face again, stroking his brown cheek with my thumb. There was saliva on his lips and I wiped it away with the towel. He seemed like the only thing I had left in the world. Jesus Christ, wisest of the wise, what am I supposed to do? Please help me.

"Take your time, Christina, it's an important decision," the doctor said.

"What about my buds here?" I asked. "They're family too."

"Who? Who are you talking about? Can anyone here take care of you like I'm going to take care of you? It's us now, Christina, don't you see that? We care about you—you and Bennie."

If I was being straight with myself, he had the skinny. C.W. didn't need me any more; it was hard to believe, but he really didn't. Trajan?—I wanted to be a million miles away from him, and, anyway, God might forsake Plentiful if it became an evil place under his control. And if the clinic closed, what was I going to do? I'd probably have to work in the kitchen day and night.

Then I thought about that red-haired soprano for a long moment.

"Well? What do you think?" Bosco asked.

"What about the guard in front?"

"He's with us. He hates it here," Bosco answered.

"When you gonna ditch?" I asked.

"Right now," Dr. Merrithew said.

"For real?"

"Yes, for real."

Bennie moved in my lap. He was mega-helpless, more helpless than the butterflies outside, and I knew I didn't have anything to fill his tummy, or even a clean diaper. Pribble—goofy, wingnut Pribble, what's gonna happen to you? And Kenny Wayne, did you ever know I was crushin on ya?

"OK, Dr. Merrithew. OK, I'm pretty sure I'm talkin sense. I'll bail."

Dr. Merrithew nodded, "Good." He stood up, ready to rip, tapping the table with his fingers. "Well, unfortunately the tram's the only way over, isn't it? Bosco, let's go talk with our friend out front."

"Alright," Bosco replied.

"But, Bosco, again, let's mingle a bit and use this Miracle-of-the-White-Winged-Dove thing as cover, but then we have to jump on it, just like we discussed."

"Don't patronize me, Doctor, I know what we talked about," Bosco said, opening the door to go. "And I got the keys to the getaway car, remember?"

"What do you want me to do?" I asked helplessly.

"Just bring Bennie and be quiet," the doctor replied.

So we left the house and moved out to the Boardwalk. I couldn't believe it, but if anything there were more butterflies than before, and I had to duck and keep my hands up to avoid Bennie becoming a landing pad for the flying things. A few people passed us in the street—mostly greens from the Riverside gang—but they all seemed to be hurrying down to the cliffs to join the others. So, with Dr. Merrithew pretending to be all fascinated by the Nature around us, pointing at this and that, we moved up to the main building, trying to act like we had some normal reason for going there. "Be slow," the doctor warned under his breath.

The building was spotted with butterflies, like some crazy paint job. I looked over my shoulder at Trajan's house across the street. I stared at the windows, praying that nobody was watching us. If I ever saw his eyes, his body, again, I think I'd die.

But now it was like I was saying good-bye to everything I looked at, just like when I'd left Circleville. Driving through town that day, I'd stared out the window at the rapids in the Parquat, at the maples, the houses and bus stops, and said, Bye-bye, so long. And now this.

SHAWNTE

I don't know where they came from, but just now I looked outside and practically jumped outta my skin: The air was filled with big insects! Right then and there I decided I wasn't going down to the celebration at the cliffs. The funeral was one thing—I had to attend that—but going outside with all those furry things buzzing around, maybe touching my face, that shit was bananas! What if they were poisonous? Nobody knew.

I settled my bones down against the kitchen wall, where I could see the door through the sheet. Some folks were still inside milling around, so I kept real quiet because I didn't want anyone asking why I was hiding out. Then the big doors opened, sending a flash of light across the floor. I couldn't see real clear, but people were leaving and arriving at the same time.

"You coming down?" a voice asked.

"Yea, in a second, but I gotta watch these folks."

"You need help with them?"

"No, don't worry about us, we need to get some things for the baby. Did Trajan leave?"

"Yea, he went to see Charles."

"Cool."

I turned my head and looked close. It was Feelgood with some others. What were they snooping around for?

The voice kept on, "Hey, ain't you the doctor from the clinic?"

"That's me."

"You got anything for tape worm? I'm so hungry, I think I got something eating my insides."

"You and me both. Listen, come by tomorrow for an exam, OK?"

"Sure thing. Well, gotta go. May Jesus be with you."

"Thank you," the doctor said.

The man left in another blast of sunlight, followed by darkness. It was quiet as a cave now and I knew the visitors figured they were all alone. There was a lot of hot whispering about something, then I heard the doctor's bugged-out voice, "I don't care, it's not important, just hurry." Then the door opened and closed again, leaving nothing but the ga-ga sounds of the baby, then some crying.

"Christina, get him to stop," the doctor insisted. "He can't do that outside."

"OK, but I gotta walk him around then."

I stiffened up. I didn't want that little bitch finding her manager all sprawled out in the dark. I peeked at her walking back and forth with the baby. Good, I thought, there's too much stuff all over the floor for her to come my way.

Just then there was a loud rumbling sound. I could feel the vibration on my back through the building wall. It was the gondola. Why, I'll be damned, are they trying to escape? I got up on my hands and knees to see better, then froze when I heard some Wild West shooting going on outside. This is my moment! Right here and now I can make my name by warning Trajan.

Then, bam, the door flew open.

"Go—run for it!" a voice demanded, and the doctor and Christina split out into the brightness.

I got my dogs movin and kicked my way through the mess on the floor, but when I got to the door I remembered the insects and my skin turned creepy. Come on girl I urged myself, bite the bullet and be a stand-up nigga. Half-closing my eyes, I pulled the door open, took a deep breathe, and hightailed it for the cliffs.

CHRISTINA

As we ran around the corner of the building, Dr. Merrithew threw his crutches down and was moving so fast that I thought he was gonna leave me and Bennie behind. But then he turned back, pulling me by the arm. "I'm coming, I'm coming!" I yelled.

Up ahead, the gondola was growling super loud (it had to be a total giveaway!) and Bosco and the guardian were scrambling around on the platform. They bent down and pushed a body off it. It landed on the ground, wasted, bleeding. I almost turned around right then and there, but the guardian, who was kneeling beside the gondola, warned, "Get your butts moving! They'll be here any second."

Pretending the dead body was invisible, I lifted Bennie high over my shoulder and barely made it up the steps, following the doctor inside the metal room. We stood there waiting, helpless, watching the butterflies float like confetti in the air outside. My body just vibrated with fear. What am I doing? I thought. Am I crazy?

"God damn it, Bosco, why ain't we movin?" the guardian screamed towards the engine room. Bosco yelled something back that I couldn't understand.

The doctor got in my face, putting his hands on my shoulders. "Christina, listen to me, if they try to stop us, show them Bennie, OK?" he said, real genuine-like. "You know they won't hurt him, so just step out there and show them. They'll understand."

143

Show Bennie? I couldn't catch his drift. But just then I heard voices outside; it was the community showing up.

"They caught us," I said to the doctor.

He immediately ducked down and crawled across the floor to the open door.

"Watch it, you two, they're out there," he yelled out to the platform.

Then there was shooting—the FLAFLAFLAFLAFLA that I'd heard at the bank, then DUKDUKDUKDUK thuds all around. The doctor, down on all fours, looked back at me, waving his hand. "Christina, come here," he insisted.

I looked at him, shaking my head, No.

"Go out there and hold Bennie up high. They'll stop attacking." Stand up there with Bennie while they were shooting at us? Was this guy outta his mind?

"Christina, are you listening to me?"

I just ignored him, holding the baby tight. Fahgettabout im, Bennie.

"Bosco?" the doctor called out. A few moments went by, then Bosco answered, "I'm pinned down. They're all over the place."

"Is—the—engine—OK?" the doctor asked.

"Yea, no damage. Let's go for it."

The doctor continued, "Guard? Guard, can you hear me?" There was no response, then banging on the side of the gondola. "We're in a bad fix, Doc," the guard said. "Trajan's gonna skin me alive for this."

"Shut up and listen," the doctor spit. "You see the tanks across the field? The two brown tanks in front of the trees. You see them?"

"Yea, I see them."

"Shoot them. Shoot the tanks."

"Shoot right at them?"

"Yes, they're a big target. Bosco, can you hear me?"

"A little—talk louder."

"After he shoots the tanks, let the tram go, it's our only chance."

"OK," the guardian agreed, "here goes."

"Do it, fill them with bullets," the doctor urged.

I closed my eyes, trying to change my world . . . *It was the most beautiful Christmas tree ever . . . With reindeer ornaments and gingerbread woodcutters . . . All wrapped in a string of popcorn with a shining angel on top . . . Gifts—*

Then, from just outside, FLAFLAFLAFLAFLA, then again FLAFLAFLA—

BOOM BOOM, the air cracked in half.

My head snapped back and Bennie almost flew outta my arms. There was a roar and people screaming—screaming like I'd never heard people scream before—then the voices disappeared into more noise and explosions. Just then, the gondola jerked and started moving forward. I don't know why, but I grabbed a hand-rail and pulled myself up, keeping my balance because the gondola was swaying.

Jesus Almighty, I thought, terrified.

Everything had gone totally berserk in an instant. The trees and the field were on fire, people running around crazy in the black smoke, some even—some—I lost my breath and collapsed down onto the floor with Bennie. Dr. Merrithew was on the floor too, his hands over his head, covered with pine needles that had just blown in. But he still got up on all fours and pushed the door shut. Of course, this kept Bosco and the guardian out, and as the gondola moved along the platform, they ran beside us, freaked out and banging on the windows.

"They're trying to get in!" I yelled at the doctor.

"Forget it, it's too late," Dr. Merrithew shot back, his hands still on the door handle.

I could see right into the men's faces. The guardian stumbled and disappeared, then Bosco—his eyes like insane laser beams—grimaced and fell away too. Then the floor got soft as the gondola floated out over the canyon. I waited for bullets, screams, but . . . nothin. I half-expected the gondola to stop and go back, but it didn't happen. We just kept going, the roaring sound—everyone and everything I knew—fading out behind us.

I closed my eyes and breathed deep, just trying to calm down. My neck was hurting from holding Bennie, so I changed positions and pulled the towel off his face. He was still as a doll. Did he faint from the explosion? A chill ran down my back. I shook him a little bit, but he didn't move. I called his name, Bennie? Bennie? Bennie? then he finally opened his eyes. Oh, you sweet guy I thought thankfully, the Lord's looking after you! He sucked on his fingers, tears running down his cheeks, then he let out a big sigh. I loosened the towel a bit so he could move better, stroking his hair with my shaking hand. But Dr. Merrithew's words, "Hold Bennie up high," kept ringing in my ears. Jeez, that pissed me off.

"I think we're almost clear," the doctor said, relieved, but still checking the island. "There isn't any organized resistance. Whether we make it all the way across is anyone's guess, but I think we escaped the worst of it." Then, like he discovered a new agenda, he spun around on the slippery metal floor and peeked out towards the other side of the canyon. "Would you look at that?" he said. "Falmouth here I come."

"What is it?" I asked, struggling to get back up again to look out across the canyon.

The other side was still a long ways away, but I could see all the people and vehicles the doctor was talking about. The whole field had become a parking lot, and as we got closer and closer, all the people started running away and hiding.

"Down, get down—they think we're attacking!" Dr. Merrithew warned, but I was so spaced out that I just kept looking. "We're getting close now," he said, "but we're moving too fast. Can we stop this thing?" I didn't have a clue or really care, waiting for whatever.

"Watch it, Christina," the doctor yelled, ducking down, "get ready to roll." But no crash ever happened. There was just a long screeching metal sound underneath us, then the gondola slowly came to a stop. It was strangely quiet. We knew they were out there, and they knew we were in the gondola, but nothing happened.

"Hold on," the doctor said in a low voice, "let's not do anything rash."

Wiped out, I sat back onto the floor with Bennie, too frightened to cry. We waited for what seemed like five or ten minutes. I killed the time blowin cool air on the baby's face, but, inside everything, one idea kept repeating in my skull: Was the fire, the whole disaster, my fault? Did I cause it?

Then a fuzzy mechanical voice started talking, "You are surrounded by the police and the National Guard. You have illegally trespassed on private land and evidently have caused harm to that private property. Surrender by coming out with your hands above your head. Keep your hands above your head or you will be regarded as dangerous."

Dr. Merrithew slid the door back. Right then, I couldn't, no matter how hard I tried, lift up Bennie and stand up. I just couldn't do it.

"I'll hold him for you" the doctor said, seeing that I was out of it.

"Yea, go ahead," I said. But after taking the baby, Dr. Merrithew just stepped through the doorway without me. Of all the crazy shit!

The voice started up again, "You are surrounded by the police and National Guard. Surrender by . . . " So, when I finally got vertical, I slowly moved out onto the platform too.

"Please, don't shoot. We just escaped," the doctor called out, raising Bennie up like some weird shield. "I'm Dr. Collin Merrithew, and we're no threat to anyone. We just escaped." Then what seemed like a hundred people started coming out from behind all the vehicles and tents. In no time, soldiers—real soldiers with gas masks, guns, spotted uniforms and black boots—were all over the platform and inside the gondola. After checking us from head to toe, we got led down the steps. I couldn't believe it, but a bunch of men with cameras on tripods took our picture as we moved across the field to a white trailer with a big antenna spinning on top.

Waiting at the trailer door, Dr. Merrithew said, "Here, take the baby back." And—Yea, thank you very much—I grabbed Bennie as fast as I could. It felt soooo good to feel his warm glow in my arms again.

"You must be happy to be going home, huh?" I said to him, still miffed at his attitude. "Happy to be taking bike rides again." But he didn't say anything, and just stared at me like I was some sort of freak. Now that we'd left Plentiful, now that we were safe, I think he saw who I really was—a poor little nobody from the wrong side of the river—and I saw who he was—a big-shot doctor—and it made us both scratch our heads. I realized he probably had a home to go to out in the estates, where everyone had big swimming pools and security guards. What'd I have in my sitch? Nothing, nothing with a capital N. Down deep, I knew I didn't even have Bennie. I wasn't his mom, only his pretend mom. Pretty much pretend everything.

A soldier standing near us looked towards Plentiful. "I can smell the smoke," he said, and I followed his eyes out past all the military trucks, out to the fire across the canyon. It was like some lost Indian tribe was sending messages across the sky.

SUZANNE

The door of the communications trailer opened and a soldier stepped inside. Everybody at the table—Bender from the FBI, the National Guard's unit commander, a shrink named Dr. Farmington, reps and attorneys from the mayors offices in Falmouth and Circleville, and us local police—had been eagerly awaiting news, and we all turned our heads in unison in hopes of a breakthrough.

"What's the status of things?" Colonel Wyler, who'd been leading the briefing, asked the soldier.

"Sir, two people—a man and a young lady—were on that transport system. They're waiting outside," the soldier announced.

"Any threat identified?" the colonel asked in all his gray-haired wonder.

"No, sir. Looks like they were just escaping—but, sir, they brought a baby along too."

"A baby? Ah, humbug, things are always more complicated with babies in the picture. Private, tell everyone we'll be out in a moment. Dismissed."

"Yes, sir," the soldier said, saluting crisply then leaving.

The colonel, who'd been standing in front of an aerial photograph we'd been analyzing, put his pencil on the easel and sat down.

148

"Well, this is a fortunate turn of events. We now actually have someone from the Byzantium encampment to talk to. Getting some leads from these people will go a long way in dealing with this crisis. Since there's a girl and a baby involved, Lieutenant Dunkirk, you go first—we need a woman's touch here. Then we'll follow up with Mr. Bender an hour later. Lieutenant, does that sound good?"

"Yes, Colonel Wyler, it does," I said, trying to mask any excitement in my voice.

"Do you have any questions?" the colonel asked me.

"No, sir, I don't," I answered. "I'll get some practical information for all of us."

The colonel leaned on his forearms. "Well, if you can, see what's going on with this fire. Besides all this human stuff, there's the forest to think about, so just relax and be informal, we'll get to audio and video later."

"Understood," I said. I stood up and gathered my paperwork, then eyed all the eminent males surrounding the table, each wearing his respective dark blue or olive green uniform or business suit. "Good-bye, gentlemen, I'll give you some feedback shortly."

They nodded, wishing me luck, and I stepped away from the table and walked down to the other end of the long doublewide, where administration and the computers were located.

I opened the Falmouth Police locker and put my notebooks away, hiding my joy with a serious game face. I just stood there for a moment, fiddling with my ammunition belt, gloating. Hot damn, I thought, I hope Kowalski and the whole department have their television sets turned on. This could mean a promotion, and allow me to start barking orders of my own. But the more I listened to myself, the more fed-up I got. Here I had this critical interrogation coming up, and all I was thinking about was Officer Kowalski! Shut the fuck up, girl, I told myself, and get on task! So, standing up extra proud and tall, and focusing to the max, I exited the trailer without another thought.

Stepping outside onto the landing, I was startled by the noisy commotion of people and vehicles. I surveyed the soldiers holding the detainees at the bottom of the stairs, but also caught the fire out of the corner of my eye. God damn, I realized, there's five plumes of black smoke filling the sky that weren't there an hour ago.

I went down the steps and introduced myself to the soldiers, then faced the pair from Byzantium: a pretty blonde, fifteen or sixteen, maybe younger, holding a baby, and a short brown-haired man.

"Hello, I'm Lieutenant Dunkirk," I said to the man, who immediately stepped up and shook my hand. He looked tired and dirty, with a number of facial cuts.

"I'm Dr. Collin Merrithew." Well, we meet again, Doctor, and, although I'm not sure I would have otherwise recognized you, I can see you're still sporting that red cycling outfit! He looked me closely in the eyes, but, no, he didn't seem to recognize me.

"It's good to meet you," I said politely, trying, without success, to catch the mean, wayward eye of the female next to him. "There are a variety of law enforcement and military groups covering this crisis," I said by way of introduction. "So, as we talk, I'll be representing all those groups."

But the doctor didn't seem to care. "I practice in Falmouth, at the About Face Institute at the Eugenia Flowers Memorial Hospital," he announced. Rather than respond, I moved in front of the girl, checking the baby she was carrying, but the doctor got in my face again. "I was kidnapped Saturday evening on the highway east of Circleville. Do—"

I cut him short, "Dr. Merrithew, we've known about your disappearance for a number of days. How are you managing things?"

He smiled, happy to have achieved some recognition. "I'm relieved to be here, to say the least. A little battered and banged up, but relieved nonetheless. We should talk and I'll give you all the details about what's been going on over there."

"Yes, we'll get to that immediately," I said, but then he touched my arm, which I thought was a bit much, saying, "But Lieutenant, can I first make a phone call? I have a medical practice, a family."

I gave him my ironclad law enforcement smile. "In a moment, Doctor, please."

I turned to the girl again. "Hi, what's your name?" Her green eyes flashed at me.

"Christina, ma'am."

"Any last name?"

"No ma'am, not that I can remember."

I looked at her, narrowing my eyes just to be funny. "Never tell your last name to the cops, is that it? Well, I don't know who taught you that, but see if I care. How are you feeling, Christina? Are you OK?"

"Totally balm," she said, smiling a little Barbie smile. What a gorgeous, proud creature she was.

"Is that your baby?" I asked.

She nodded, Yes.

"What's his name?"

"Bennie."

"That's a nice name. Like the Elton John song. You know, Christina, we have a nurse if you need any help."

The girl hid the boy's face in a towel. "No," she demanded in a rush of paranoia. "Don't even try to touch him."

"That's fine, honey, nobody's trying to take him from you. But is he thirsty or wet?"

Before the poor, disheveled thing could respond, Dr. Merrithew tapped me on the shoulder again. "Excuse the young lady—we've been through a lot. The fact is, we need something to eat and drink. A cup of coffee would be ideal."

"That can be arranged, no problem. Soldiers, accompany these newcomers to the blue tent. Dr. Merrithew, there's a cafeteria inside and restrooms next door. Get whatever you like, then we can talk in more detail about your experiences."

But Christina raised the baby up on her shoulder and shook her head defiantly. "What is this, Greeting the Chameleon? Why don't you just send me and the baby back over."

"Will you calm down?" Dr. Merrithew said impatiently. "She's trying to help."

"Help me? This robot? Helloooo, I doubt—" But her words were swamped by a thumping, ear-splitting sound. We all turned towards the racket and saw a helicopter hovering above the trees. It hung in the air, propeller beating, then slowly dropped down, landing at the far end of the field, blowing rocks and leaves everywhere.

I yelled orders in a soldier's ear, and he ushered the detainees over to the blue tent and disappeared inside. I watched as two men with cameras, clothes blown back, eyes squinting, ran out and climbed into the helicopter. The mechanical beast slowly did its levitating thing then tilted forward and flew out over the canyon, leaving my ears ringing.

I rushed over to the medical unit and arranged for an emergency medical technician—a gentleman named Charles Yu—to accompany me back to the cafeteria with some practical things for the baby. I warned him to lie low and not make the young lady more defensive than she already was. I believed she knew a lot more about the encampment than the doctor, and, if possible, I wanted her trust during the interrogation.

Inside, the cafeteria was quiet and still, except for a group of jarheads eating at a long table. Passing the men, I said, "Sorry soldiers, but on Colonel Wyler's orders, you'll need to leave. I have to conduct some official business here." Still chewing food and guzzling drinks, the young men obediently got up and left.

The doctor and girl were standing over by the food line, so the EMT and I walked over and set the baby's things on a nearby table.

". . . dive in, Christina," Dr. Merrithew was saying, holding a cup of coffee and eating a banana. "There's burgers and fries, and mashed potatoes and meatloaf, but don't expect any Wonder Wraps."

The girl, holding the baby like her life depended on it, sat down, scowling. "The smell's making me sick," she complained, giving me the once over. "What's Strike Force mean, anyway?" she asked, referring to the lettering across my shirt.

"That's the special group I'm in at the police department."

"Wow," she said sarcastically. Although I liked her spunk, I knew this tattooed smart aleck was nothing but Youth Authority bait. I introduced Mr. Yu to her, then suggested he take a seat and relax. "I brought you some things," I said, trying to spark Christina's enthusiasm. I opened up a bag and spread out some Pampers, a change of clothes, a milk bottle, and a couple rattles.

"What's that there?" she asked, pointing at the plastic bassinet.

I slid it in front of us. "See, you can put Bennie in here if you want to change him," I explained.

"It looks like the snow sled we'd take up to Zimmer Grade."

"Want me to show you how to use it?"

"Not a chance. I can do it myself," the girl insisted. She stood up and slowly put Bennie down in the dish. He immediately burst into a feverish wail, his nose all snotty.

"Christina, is the baby hot? Does he have a fever?"

The girl blushed. No, she nodded, obviously lying.

"Can I touch his forehead and see?"

"No—don't. I mean, maybe you can sometime, but not right now."

"But Christina, we have medical—"

"I don't know you," she said, gritting her teeth. "Get it?"

"OK . . . OK, I understand loud—"

"Ms. Dunkirk?" the doctor interrupted. I hadn't noticed him standing right next to us. "That baby has bronchitis and a 103 temperature," he said, taking a bite of Danish, then a coffee chaser. "I'm sure, with your law enforcement training, you know just the steps to remedy the situation."

I thought: don't one up me, you bastard. I just ignored him, keeping an eye on the girl. "See, Christina, the doctor here can help with his advice too," I said.

Christina looked at me, her eyes filled with some anger I couldn't understand. "You're joking, right?" she said. Shaking her head in frustration, she unfolded the makeshift diaper from around the baby's skinny brown hips, and, yep, it stunk to high heaven. Christina didn't really know what to do with the mess. She picked up a Pamper like it was a foreign object, but suddenly stopped, confused and internalized. I'd been undecided, but as each moment passed with her helplessly standing there, I became more and more convinced she needed a psych evaluation.

"You do it," she finally said, and so, gratefully, I stepped in and started my smelly chores, which I was all too familiar with after changing Ferdinand a thousand times the past two years. I tossed the makeshift diaper into the trash, wiped the screaming banshee clean, then fit him into a new diaper and a loose pair of yellow pajamas. But when I picked up the milk bottle for Bennie, Christina took offense and wedged herself in front of me.

"I'll do it," she insisted.

"Fine—here," I said, handing her the bottle. "Put it in his hands," I advised, "he'll do the rest." She knew it would do the baby good, but still waited a long skeptical moment before letting his tiny hands grip the bottle. The moment Bennie took it, his eyes got huge, his lips sucking like a rabbit.

"You really love that baby, don't you?" I commented.

She just looked at him shyly, pushing her long hair out of her face. "Ma'am, there's one thing you gotta promise me."

"What's that, Christina?"

"Don't take Bennie away, OK?"

"Well—"

"Back in Circleville, when this is over, visiting rights, OK? I just want to be able to see him."

"Let's just be patient, we have a lot to do before then."

"Bennie would be sad without me, you know? He needs me."

"I understand."

"Dunkirk?" the doctor interrupted again. "It's not her baby. Do you realize that?"

Christina claimed she was the mother, but when I looked at her for confirmation, her face didn't reveal a thing. Shit, I thought, Colonel Wyler's words of wisdom are coming back to haunt me.

"We won't go there right now, Doctor. Are you ready to talk?"

"I've been ready."

"Over in the corner, where that small table is," I suggested. I touched Christina's shoulder, letting her know I was leaving. Keeping her eyes lowered, she warned, "Don't believe nothin he say's about Plentiful. He doesn't know the story and he's a liar."

So that's what they called Byzantium: Plentiful. "Well, young lady, you can give me the whole scoop when we talk later, OK?"

"Me?" she asked, looking up, scowling.

"Yes, you." I insisted, winking at her.

Just then, the tent door opened and a man with a camera on his shoulder, wires hanging to his waist, and a tall brunette dressed in a red business suit, stepped inside. There'd been such community

154

hysteria in Falmouth after the Path of Peace crime spree that Colonel Wyler insisted we give full media access during operations, so I let the reporters into a fray I knew was best kept private.

"Right over here," I said, pointing to Christina and the baby. I noticed the doctor quickly turned his back and slipped away to the corner. "But you have to be quick," I reminded them. The cameraman hustled over and knelt down, panning the interior. I crossed my arms and let him get a long, dignified shot of me alone, then I stood behind Christina at the table for some more coverage. That should get me in the limelight, I thought confidently.

"Can you look this way, please?" the reporter asked Christina, but, true to form, she ducked down and hid her head between her legs. The woman looked at me in frustration. "Can you get her attention? I have some questions for her."

"No, absolutely not. You can interview me later if you want, but it has to be outside."

"That's not what we were told. I need a quick introduction taken—"

"No, no, no. Both of you—out," I said, walking over to the door. "I'll give you the time you want, but only if you do as I say." The reporter, who I knew was one of those ice queens who never wanted to be delayed in anything she did, gave me a hard look as she walked out, cameraman in tow.

After I coaxed Christina into raising her head up again, I told her to talk to Mr. Yu if she needed anything, then walked over to the little table where Dr. Merrithew was waiting. I was tempted to pull out my little tape recorder, but I decided to forgo the prop and just face the man.

As I sat down, he said, "I remember you now—and that afternoon." I laughed, and, although I knew it was unprofessional, laughed again. "It just goes to show, Doctor, you shouldn't run from the law."

He stared at me coldly. "Let's get down to business."

"Yes, let's."

"It's a cult, if you need to know," he said.

I folded my hands and breathed deep. I glanced at Christina and was surprised to find her talking with the EMT. "What do you mean, a Christian cult?" I asked.

"A bit Christian, a bit street with some leftist politics thrown in, just one of those absurd New World Utopia things."

"Well, who's the girl? Is she related to you?"

"Related to me? No, she's not related to me! What gave you that idea?"

"Just asking, no problem. Who is she then?"

"Just one of the refugees from Circleville—same with the baby. But they have nothing to do with me."

"What's the baby's identity?"

"I don't know."

"Do you know their names?"

"Well, yea, Christina and Bennie, other than that I couldn't tell you. I was thrown in with a couple hundred people and the three of us ended up together, just lucky enough to escape."

"Dr. Merrithew, the entire Byzantium mine is on fire. We can't even get close enough to land any personnel. Do you know what happened?"

"Again, I was there such a short time, I honestly couldn't tell you."

"Was there discussion of any ritual suicide, anything of that sort?"

"When I think back, it may have been alluded to at some of the meetings. Their leader—"

"Charlton Jokelson?"

"Charlton—yes, he went by C.W. He was into an apocalyptic kind of thing—Us against the World—and he could very well have started the fire."

"OK, when would that have been, and how did he do it?"

"I have no idea."

"Did you ever talk with Jokelson?"

"Yea, I talked with him. We talked a couple times. He needed a doctor, so he took special interest in me."

"What did he say?"

"What didn't he say. He's a very manic guy, intelligent, but in way over his head."

"Did you know him before?"

"He's not my type, Dunkirk."

I'd heard Charlton Jokelson's name in briefings for so many years, and seen the video clips from the demonstrations and the acts of civil disobedience and the crazy TV interviews so many times, I was surprised the doctor was unaware of his notoriety.

"How did you end up over there?"

"You know, I'm almost too embarrassed to say. That same day when I was on my bike, I took a spill up in the hills and injured my ankle. Look—" He shifted in his seat and lifted up his foot to me; his lower leg was seriously discolored. "To get help, I accepted a ride from these people, but instead of taking me to a hospital, they forced me up here. But my ankle needs some medical attention, and, as I said before, I have to make a phone call to Falmouth ASAP."

"That's no problem, Dr. Merrithew, I have a cell phone and you're welcome to use it when we're done. But first things first. Plentiful—what do the authorities here need to know?"

"Like I said, a couple hundred people. There are automatic weapons. But basically it's a hodgepodge of desperate street folk who are running out of food and water. With the fire, I don't know what's going on at ground zero over there."

"Do you know of any other way to get—"

"Excuse me, Lieutenant Dunkirk . . . " It was the EMT.

"Yes, what is it, Mr. Yu?"

"I'm sorry for interrupting, but that baby really needs to go to the infirmary right away. He's throwing up the milk, and he's very short of breath. He needs, at the very least, some antibiotics . . . "

"Thanks for letting me know," I said.

"Dunkirk, that's exactly what I was saying. The baby's ill and malnourished. Why are you procrastinating?"

"I'm not procrastinating, Dr. Merrithew—not now. We need to finish our talk, but let me deal with this first."

When I stood up, Christina looked at me from the far end of the tent. She had antenna a mile long and I could tell she already knew what was up. I approached her, doing my best to be upbeat.

"Christina, both the medical specialists think Bennie's really sick. I need you to give me the baby now and we'll take him over to the infirmary, alright?"

She stood up slowly. "I knew it! I knew you were gonna trick me," she taunted.

"No, that's not—"

"My parents, they—you're gonna put him in a child prison, aren't you? I know what that is, do you? Huh, do you?"

"—you can see Bennie after he recovers, Christina."

"Nooooo," she said, pulling the milk bottle out of Bennie's mouth. Then she turned and threw the bottle at me, and just for good measure, swept everything off the table with her arm, the stuff scattering all over the floor. OK, I thought, be a crazed animal protecting your young. I know you're expecting brute force, but I'm going to disappoint you. Mr. Yu came up beside me and the soldier by the door moved closer. "Be ready you two," I ordered.

As I stepped towards Christina, she picked up the baby in the basinet and moved back into the corner. She set the basinet on the floor and stood in front of it. She was near the start of the foodline and, looking around nervously, she grabbed a long serving fork and turned and faced me, wielding it like a sword. "Get away," she warned. "I'll rip you apart."

"Sweetheart, I know you've been through a lot at Plentiful—"

"Shut up, liar. God will punish you, bitch liar!"

"Think of the baby, Christina, think of—"

"I have something to say! I have something to say!" she announced, standing at attention. She looked over towards Dr. Merrithew in the corner. "Is everyone ready? I got the truth to tell."

I sat down at a table, trying to defuse things, and motioned for Mr. Yu to do the same. "Take your time now," I said in my calmest voice. "What is it you want to tell us?"

She pointed at the doctor with the long fork. "He did it. He set the fire."

"The fire at the mine?" I asked.

"Yea, he burned down Plentiful, then got out."

I glanced at the doctor. He just glared at his coffee cup, turning it in circles.

Christina kept on: "Shoot the gas tanks, he said. Shoot the gas tanks. Yea, they got shot all right. So help me God, I'm not lying,

I was there. And the butterflies . . . Oh, all the butterflies—please, Jesus, forgive me. Forgive me. Forgive me."

As she stopped talking, her eyes focused on the doctor. Slowly, like a shadow, an infuriated look passed over her face, then she burst towards him. Without thinking, I jumped up and blocked her way, and for a few seconds I had to keep my hands up, shielding myself from the fork and her scratching fingers. But, as quickly as she'd attacked, she just stopped, looked me sadly in the eye, and fainted, collapsing hard to the ground before I could catch her.

ESTELLE

"I never knew you liked apple sauce so much," Sophie said sweetly, giving me another spoonful. What a sister! After all the turmoil, she was still faithfully by my side.

"I like the cinnamon on top," I said, collapsing back and putting my hand up, not wanting any more.

Sophie put the plastic container down. "Will this storm ever quit?" she asked, glancing out the hospital window at the gray sky. "Maybe I should have moved to Falmouth years ago, just like you recommended,"

"Chicago fits you fine, Fifi," I said. "No need to share my . . . situation."

Sophie held my hand. "I love you," she said, "and everything's going to be just fine."

"What did the shrink say?"

"You're on hold for seventy-two hours."

I breathed deep, shaking my head. "Just for talking about it?"

"Well, yes, they felt you were serious."

"I was."

"Estelle, let's forget all that. It's in the past now. You have so much to live for. You're beautiful, intelligent . . . "

"And childless."

She squeezed my hand harder. "Yes, and childless, but that's just the way it is. And that can change in the future, you know. You're not neutered like me."

I tipped my head back and looked at the white floating ceiling. "I'm not sure if it was even the abortion that made me talk that way. It was more . . . not being able to decide . . . being so spineless and uncertain. Why?"

"Well, unlike me, you've always had too many options, too many talents. It's makes it hard, Estelle."

"Don't be ridiculous. I've got a rich husband and a big house. That's my expertise."

"Does the medication make you feel better?"

"I'm more relaxed."

"You look better. You have some color in your cheeks," Sophie said. "Just remember, this sounds kind of gross, but flowers do grow out of manure, so just learn from your mistakes, OK?"

Then came that insidious snake hiss melody of her cell phone.

"I'll turn it off," she said, reaching for her purse.

"No, don't—"

"But it's such a nuisance."

"If it's Collin, I want to talk."

She checked the Caller ID. "Well, it's your area code, but it's not a good idea right now, Estelle. You need to wait a few—"

"Fifi, I'll never speak to you again, and I'm being decisive—very decisive—about this."

She stood up. "He needs to know what's happened," she said.

"Don't worry, I'll tell him what he needs to know."

Sophie put the cell phone to her ear. "Hello," she said. "Well, if it isn't the wayfaring doctor. What's up? Is she? Yes, Estelle's still here. But don't be long, OK? She needs her sleep."

Sophie handed me the phone and with great effort I straightened up against the pillows. I could see my disheveled image reflected in a large mirror along the opposite wall. OK, I thought desperately, dive in.

"Collin," I said.

"Hello Estelle. If you can't hear me very well, it's because I'm up in the mountains. Why?—that's a whole long story I'll have to tell you about. How are you feeling? Are you recuperating alright?"

160

"The baby's a goner, Collin, if that's what you're asking?"

"Well, partly. Why are you still in—"

"Collin," I interrupted.

"Yes, I'm here, do you want to say something?"

Do I want to say something? Well, do I? I panicked for a second and looked at Sophie for support, but she was staring out the window. I caught my image in the mirror again. It stared back at me, waiting impatiently.

"Collin," I said again.

"I'm waiting, Estelle. Why are you—"

"I want a divorce, Collin. I'm calling an attorney and divorcing you. Is that clear? I'll talk to you when I get back. Don't call here again because I won't talk with you and there's no debating this. I have nothing more to say to you. Good-bye."

I dropped the cell phone and it crashed to the floor. Then I scooted down and snuggled under the covers. I looked at Sophie: She continued to gaze at the rainy day outside, a little Mona Lisa smile on her face.

BARBARA

I heard the phone ringing in my office and rushed down the hall to answer it. "Ms. Eastwood speaking," I said, out of breath.

"Barbara, Collin here."

"Yes! I prayed I'd be hearing your voice soon. Are you OK?"

"I'm up in the mountains—"

"I phoned the police and made a full report."

"Good! I was able to escape and I'm here in the forest with the authorities."

"You got out of that place safe and sound?"

"Yes, it was an ordeal, but I did it."

"I can't believe it! What wonderful news. I've been sending out positive thoughts to you day and night. I have to tell everybody."

"Well, hold on first. Listen, what happened to our pet project."

"Ms. Magliori's staying in New York for the time being. I told her manager about waiting until the end of the week, or maybe next week, and he had a fit. He said he would call back when she'd decided her plans. When are you going to be available?"

"I don't know exactly . . . Barbara?"

"Yes, Doctor."

"How have you been? Busy?"

"Well, not as busy as when you're here."

"Throughout this whole thing, I've had so much time to think. Do you have any idea how much I depend on you?"

"Well, I've always tried to do a good job for you—"

"No, I mean more than that. You've always been my biggest supporter, and I want you to know how much I appreciate that. I truly care for you, not just as a secretary, but as a human being, and as a woman."

I sat down at my desk, blushing, even though I was alone. Can what I'm hearing be true? Has this man done some soul-searching and finally realized what a diamond in the rough I really am?

"Well, thank you Doctor, I'm flattered. I've always respected you, and, if the truth be known, cared for you too."

"Let's talk more about it sometime. But Barbara, right now I need some help on things outside of the clinic. Estelle's not available."

"I fed the dogs. I know that sounds crazy, but I went up to Buckwood Estates and took care of that yesterday. I figured those poor spaniels would be suffering with nobody there, and I didn't know if the housekeeper was coming around or not."

"That's a relief, thank you. Do anything at the house that you think needs to be done, OK? You have carte blanche. Even take a sauna if you like. But I do need you to call my personal attorney immediately. His number is in my Rolodex under K. It's Bart Kraven at Twilly, Kraven & Jones. Tell him to expect a call from me in the next day or so. Tell him he has to be available."

"OK. Can I ask why?"

"It's a long story. It's become complicated up here with this cult. I'm being asked questions and all sorts of things."

"Will you be in tomorrow?"

"You know, I'm not sure. They're holding me."

"Holding you?"

"Barbara, just contact Mr. Kraven. I'll call him when I get back to Falmouth."

"I never called Estelle, just like you said."

"That's fine. I talked with her."

"Is she having a good time with Jackson?"

"She's having the time of her life. I have to go. I really look forward to seeing you when I get back to the valley. I miss the clinic."

"You sweet guy. You know I'll be here, so just let me know."

"Will do. *Ciao*."

CHRISTINA

I opened my eyes. I thought for a moment I was in the clinic with Ruth, but then realized I was majorly confused. I musta gone blotto after Bennie was taken away.

I sat up and looked around at the medical equipment and beds, touching my sore arm and shoulder. I was in a different tent now.

"Well, how are you feeling?" a voice asked. I pushed my hair out of my face and looked at a woman with long blonde pigtails. Her tag said Registered Nurse.

I rubbed my face. "My heads exploding," I complained.

"Yes, you fainted. You might have landed on it."

My mouth was super dry, but I waved off the cup of soup the nurse offered me, suspicious of what might be in it. Why'd I have this life anyway? I thought sorrowfully. Why can't I just sleep forever?

"Where's Bennie?" I asked.

"I'm sorry, who?"

"The baby."

"Yes, of course. He was evacuated to Eugenia Flowers Memorial."

"On Bridgeway Drive?"

"Yes, the hospital in Falmouth. He was a sick little guy."

Sweet Bennie, you prisoner, what's going to happen to you now?

There was a bunch of booming sounds outside, like thunder or cannons.

Plentiful—the lost city of Plentiful. The sounds kept repeating, and, as I listened closely to them, my thinking got clearer and clearer. If it's history, it's history, so go make history. I repeated the words again, slower this time: If it's history, it's history, so go make history. Now I kinda understood what C.W. meant by that silly saying. I'd always been the one who knew the history of "The Melopedia" and "The Golden Stories", but what did I know about the future? They'd burned down the Day-Glo Apartments, and now they'd burned down Plentiful, so history was just repeating itself, right? But what was next? What? Well, if I really loved C.W. and really loved Jesus Christ and had His power in my heart, then, yea, I had to keep all the words alive ... but more than that, I had to do something with the words. I realized right then and there that I had to pass something on to Bennie; I had to teach him everything that C.W. had taught me about life and joy and justice through Christ Almighty.

I quietly moved over to the edge of my bed, watching the nurse. She walked over to a man lying down on the other side of the tent. He said something to her and they both laughed real loud. When she bent over to adjust some equipment, I got up and tiptoed over to the door, then slowly turned the handle and slipped outside.

I squinted in the bright sunlight. I knew I was exposed like an x-ray and had to act super quick before anyone noticed I'd split, so I crept around the corner of the tent. I ran into a growling forklift and just stared at the driver's back. It started turning towards me, so I ducked behind a row of tall red containers and, crouching down, moved along until I came to a point where I could see across the field to the tall trees where I needed to go.

The back of a truck slammed shut and some soldiers carrying backpacks moved by, smoking cigarettes. I was about to jump for it, but my eye caught the door of a portable toilet opening up. A woman—Lieutenant Dunkirk!—stepped out, and climbed into a jeep and roared away. Run for it, Christina. Now! So, gritting my teeth, I busted major tail all the way across the field. When I reached the trees, I scrambled behind some bushes, crouching low, my heart pounding like a hammer. I looked back; nobody'd caught my scent yet. Now, where's the treasure? I remembered.

I went deeper into the forest, moving from one tree trunk to another, trying to get to the dirt road Pribble had taken in from the highway on our past trips to the gondola. Whoa! Two deer watched me with their glass eyes then bounced off through the woods. Slipping and sliding and bending branches back, I kept scrambling until I finally hit the road. I waited, and since there were no voices or engine sounds, I ran across it, over to the base of two big rocks. I started searching every square inch of ground around the rocks. Where are they? I wondered, starting to get pissed. Was I wrong about it? Just when I was getting down in the dumps, I saw a little glimmer of red under some dry branches. Cashola!

I pulled off the limbs, then tipped up one of the bikes. The tires? I checked with my hands—totally flat. I let the bike drop and raised up the other one and checked again—Yes, just enough air!

I decided to stay off the dirt road cause I might be spotted. There was a little rocky path that went through the trees, so I carefully rolled the bike along it, testing the brakes, which seemed to work all right. I pushed down, down, down the path, glad that I wasn't carrying Bennie, but already missing my little guy too.

Suddenly, I came out of the shadows into this open place. I realized I was up on the edge of a cliff and down below I could see, like, millions of trees for miles and miles. Flakes of black soot floated in the air like dirty snow. Then, way out there, all by itself, was Plentiful. It looked like a burning ship in the middle of the ocean, just like C.W. had said. C.W., whatever you're doing—and what was he doing now that the fire had started?—please forgive me for all I done wrong. I'll try to remember everything. And dear, sweet Jesus, please take care of the flock . . .

165

Three helicopters were flying in circles above the island and for a moment I looked close to see the cable or anyone or anything other than smoke and flames, but it was too far off. So I turned away and kept moving along with the bike; in no time, the trail dead-ended at the highway. I stood there in the gravel at the edge of the asphalt, the bike leaning against my hip, aware I was about to leave the mountains for good. Whoever's gonna catch me now better have some rippin wheels.

The wind blew through the trees and now I could smell the smoke. Almost everyone I loved, almost every memory, was in that hot thick air, and knowing that made it smell sweet to me. I breathed deeply a couple times to take it inside, then cupped my hands and spread the smoke over my face and hair, keeping it forever. Then I pictured Bennie's brown angel face, his happy eyes, his chubby hands and arms, and knew I had to get crackin to the hospital to see him. I was his only kin now, and the only one who could tell him about his mother and the Exodus from Circleville.

I rolled the bike down the highway and got on. The seat felt pretty good, although my pussy was kinda sore and my arm hurt some. I started pedaling along and for some reason remembered Kenyatta Koffee and that stupid woman trying to answer the daily question—and the doctor, who turned out to be stupid too.

But I had plenty of time to myself now, so, keeping my eyes on the road and my legs pumping hard, I decided to practice. What was that song that got interrupted the other day in the van, the one I never finished? Jeez, why can't I . . . wait, now . . . now I remember, it was "A Human Situation"!

The trees, the mountains, flashed by my face like a carnival ride as I got movin faster and faster down the highway. I crossed over the yellow centerline then weaved back and forth, free as a bird.

OK, in honor of C.W., the last part goes—

> . . . You know, the sneaky Chameleon
> That keeps us all poor and sick—
> See, you may write poems about the birds
> The bees . . . I've seen the birds and bees

The oceans . . . there are seven
The sky . . . it covers me—
But I've got a situation
A human situation
Right here in this family room
A no-food-in-the-frig, no bus fare
Baby's crying, and my feet are too sore to walk
Kind of situation
A turned off
Grandma's dying
Mother's crazy from the factory
And Papa's bent like a sword
Situation—
Yes, it's sad that beavers die in the Parquat River
Sad the herons in the wetlands fly fallow
But I've got a human situation
To change
And a sneaky Chameleon
To destroy.
I start this instant
To destroy it.

The End